THE INTERGALACTIC VETERINARIAN OF THE YEAR!

A CRUISE BROTHERS NOVEL

RON COLLINS

JEFF COLLINS

Skyfox Publishing

ISBN-10: 1-946176-55-9
ISBN-13: 078-1-946176-55-4

For Frisky

Always Our Kitty!

PROLOGUE

A standard hour before *Galactic Marvel* was due to launch, the dark shape of Secret Agent Gustave Mann stood alone in a shadowed alcove of the massive transit station.

He'd loaded the persona of an old-school detective from the library this time, simply because it felt right.

That meant he'd found himself hanging back in the shadows and leaning casually against the wall beside one of the fast-drop restaurants built on an upper level. He lifted a titanium finger to push the brim of his hat up over his fleshy skull. For an instant, he thought he wanted a cigarette—which his link told him was an ancient form of nicotine delivery that came encased in smoke.

He ignored the craving though, which was harder than he thought it might be.

"Remind me not to use the Spade profile again," he whispered to himself.

Command received and noted, the voice in his head answered.

Mann flipped switches on magnetic and bio detectors but turned them off quickly to avoid detection. Both technologies were active, which meant they could be read by others if they were ready for it.

He didn't want to tip anyone off.

Intelligence the bureau had received earlier suggested strongly that one of the passengers was a fraud, and instead of being a veterinarian, the passenger was an agent of an intergalactic crime family, here to engage in some kind of business expansion. A follow-up investigation confirmed the information was solid. An unidentified group had acquired a billet specifically to establish an inside position with the veterinarian community.

Galaxy-wide domination of a major market was supposed to be at stake, though no one seemed sure of exactly what the market might be, or why the negotiations would be happening on a cruise for veterinarians.

"They who control the beasts control the world," N'Sai, his significant other, had quipped when he explained he'd be away for two weeks, one for the tour itself, another for the debrief. Of course, she had laughed then, and that pissed him off.

She knew his career wasn't exactly taking off, but she didn't know exactly how *not taking off* it really was.

Coming back empty-handed this time could be the end of his life as a field worker.

The idea of a desk job made the metallic parts of his bones feel dead.

He couldn't have that.

Secret Agent Mann's jaw took a firm line.

His eyes—one brown and human, the other green

and *not* human—focused on the scene below. The flat flooring and curved dome of Cygnus Grand Central Station—which was well-lit but gave a transparent view of the starfield overhead—gave the station a cathedral-like aura. It echoed with voices and the grinding wheels of transport units racing over controlled paths.

With a final crunch, Secret Agent Mann tossed aside the remains of a sugary candy stick he'd picked up at one of the endless shops that lined the gateway tunnels.

Xandarian peppermint.

Total score.

The docs back at the Bureau warned him that sweets would rot the physical side of his brain, but he didn't care. He had a MIND of his own, so it didn't matter—and a secret agent's life was not everything the viddies made them out to be. He needed something to lean on in the dull moments.

A deep breath let the essence of mint flow into his lungs.

There were a *lot* of dull moments.

Exhibit A: Across the distance, the chaotic jumble of passengers traversed the long transit tubes that led to the cruiser.

He'd been here for three standard hours now, taking it all in and trying to ignore the lack of anything obvious going on.

No bad guys.

Or, at least, no cruisegoers loading into *Marvel*'s Passenger Bay entry had shown any indication of tendencies toward bad guy behaviors.

The bright white gangway frames made a good background for the holoprojections of exotic locations across the galaxy that crawled across them. The transit station's curved ceilings were made of radiation-hardened glass that gave the passengers open views of the velvety blackness of deep space around them, views which, when combined with the safari-like music that played in the background, were designed to add to the sense of adventure that came with the cruise.

Good luck with that.

GCL, the Galactic Cruise Lines, made damn sure that no real danger could exist for their precious passengers. Not while they were out on tour, anyway.

In the mix of the population, though…well, if there was anything Secret Agent Mann had figured out in his five standards of service, it was that people, no matter what sector they were from, were dangerous.

He popped another mint. MIND registered more data.

Screw the docs.

His stainless titanium teeth crunched the hard candy covering, and the synapses of his human brain sizzled in joy. The registers of his Mass Intellect Neuroplastic Driver stored away caloric and nutritional data about the candy, including the fact that it was his fifth such dose in less than an hour.

Some sidekick.

Down on the floor, the yipping snaps of barking creatures that Secret Agent Mann's registers identified as a Yorkshire terrier broke the low-grade hum that permeated the station.

A loud hiss came in return—this time from a massive Gartagian Feline Being, or GFB for short. It was something that, from the distance, looked almost like a domestic cat. That is if that cat had bulked up to ten times its weight and then crashed headfirst into a brick wall over and over again until its face, ears, and shoulders got bunched together into a single flat surface.

A GFB was more bulldog than a cat at the front end, but a hundred percent feline in the hind quarters.

Its tail was long and furry. It was a muscular beast, too, the GFB.

"Quiet down, Hack!" a human yelled at the animal as he pulled on the heavy steel leash that wrapped around the gargantuan beast's waist, chest, and forelegs —as if that would keep the GFB under control if things got truly hairy.

Other passengers carried cages that encased feathered creatures, lizardly things, or one of an endless myriad of other strange beasts Mann did not recognize.

He sneezed and scratched at a hive that was growing on his forearm.

Veterinarians, the agent thought as he sunk deeper into the shadows.

Of all the luck.

I'm finally assigned a decent case—chasing down shady crooks dealing with the Galactic Cruise Line, and now this: The Intergalactic Vet of the Year cruise.

He scratched his hive again.

The cruise's flight log said the trip would take the passengers to five of the universe's most amazing zoological compounds, including a wild safari and a sectioned-off portion of the methane oceans on Grace, a distant planet in the Canis Major system.

At least that might be interesting to see.

If he could get off the ship, anyway.

Animals were the worst, though.

They made him break out in hives.

Down on the floor, a tripodal hominid of origin Mann was not initially familiar with entered the passenger gate, hopping along beside another creature of equal size. *Rallaz kangaroo*, his MIND told him. Then his sidekick continued with a data stream that suggested the creature was named after Manjella Rallaz, a scientist who had discovered it. MIND also noted that the unfortunate Dr. Rallaz had been subsequently eaten after she found herself between the kangaroo of her legacy and a plate of mashed bangers.

Turns out the average Rallaz kangaroo has a mad passion for bland dinners.

Without having seen the tripod commanding the hominid, Secret Agent Mann wouldn't have been able to tell which of the two was the owner and who was the pet.

As if that mattered.

He scratched his shoulder, thinking about allergic reactions, then scanned the last of the passengers as they slipped through the transit and into the bay. None of them appeared outwardly suspicious, but just looking at the GFB was making him break out in more hives.

The dogs were going to make him batshit crazy. And the rest? Well.

A shiver ran down his spine.

A Denebian lumbered up the gangway, its bulging, purple-skinned neck standing out starkly against the white pullover poncho draped over its shoulders. It pulled an antigravity cart behind, also covered in a flowing drape, this one a rusted red. A beast inside gave a gurgling Whoopi cushion of a bleat that was half goat and half gastric accident.

It was a sound caustic enough that even his party-pooper of a MIND unit wasn't fast enough to stifle his guffaw.

It wasn't his fault.

Secret Agent Gustave Mann hadn't had a pet since he was six years old, and his fathers had gotten pissed off at him because he squashed all the ants in the farm they'd given him for his birthday. He'd been watching superhero shows and thought the tiny insects were people who had simply shrunk to ant size and retained their human strength.

That was before the accident.

Before he'd become this thing that he was.

Half human, half machine, and fully uncomfortable around people of all kinds.

He was only a kid then, though.

How was he supposed to know the little buggers in his farm *weren't* nano-enhanced critters like they were on the vid shows?

Chief Dispatcher AI Unit Wilx must have had an idea about his weak spot. Mann could hear the asshole chuckling to itself from parsecs away. "This cruise is a big deal!" Wilx had said while doling out the assignment, its voice wrapped in a blanket of seriousness.

To its credit, Wilx had tried to make the assignment sound benign and sincere, but Mann had sensed an overly delighted aura of one-upthemship in the way the chief dispatcher's antennae had bounced back and forth while transmitting the assignment. Mann knew what

Wilx thought of him, too. AI Unit Wilx thought Mann was overbearing and overly thoughtful in his approach. That he had difficulty getting to his points—which was an original sin to an AI, who had to sit for interminable cycles while others of flesh, blood, and wire traces got to their points.

But Mann couldn't help it if public speaking made him nervous, or that the term "public speaking" meant anytime more than two people were in a small room.

The two had been uneasy work partners since the day Mann had joined the bureau, and he didn't think he was imagining things when he felt Wilx seemed to enjoy the irony of giving Mann this assignment just a little too much.

Wilx knew a mission on a veterinarian's cruise would literally get under Mann's skin.

Could it be payback for the Henson affair?

Screw it. That had been his partner's fault.

He and AI Wilx had never really seen eye to lens, but the Henson affair seemed to be the point where the AI had gone from making jokes at his expense to full-onset passive-aggressive behaviors.

All Mann knew now was that the last of the veterinarians were loading, so it was time to get to work. He pulled his hat down over his gaze, turned on one heel, and went to find his way aboard the cruiser.

CHAPTER 1

James gave an angry stare at the deep gouge that sliced over the body of his favorite guitar. Heat flushed his cheeks. He didn't want to be here, anyway. He would, for example, have much preferred they take the cash from the *Epic* cruise and make music.

But Lyn, his twin brother, had gotten a snootful of the admiration that came from being on a big stage and had gotten adamant.

It's a great way to see the universe, James! Lyn had argued. *And if we make a name for ourselves in front of a few thousand cruisers, it can't help but add to sales when we get to the studio!*

James had capitulated, of course. Because that's what he did. He was three minutes older, and three minutes wiser. But Lyn knew how to pull his strings.

Now, however, this.

"The cat is *going* to die," he said.

He was referring to Frisky—the beefy Maltese gray warrior cat that had adopted Lyn on their last cruise.

Lyn wasn't paying attention, though.

It was Opening Night of GCL's annual *Intergalactic Vet of the Year* cruise, and the brothers were standing backstage at the Solar Winds Grand Auditorium—the cruiser's largest theater. Both wore one of the new body-suits Lyn had found in Ellen's, an upscale shop he'd found in Dazzle Plaza, a loosely connected set of shops and boutiques tucked away in places only the connected would know about—all specializing in ultra-modern cosmic couture. The fabric of the suits clung tightly to their bodies. Quantumly Networked Piezoelectric threads ran through each of the garments and interacted with both the boys' movements and the sonic fields around them to create light displays that changed colors and patterns in response to the music they played.

The outfits cost most of their advance, but even with his general malaise about the gig, James had to admit they were stunning.

Just strumming an open chord sent a mesmerizing rainbow of sound over James's hip, and given that the fabric had a sensory aspect to it, the vibration made for an interesting feedback loop.

Lyn peered over the gathering audience.

The veterinarians had packed the place. Voices rumbled in the acoustically perfect space, and passengers milled about with an energy that surprised them both.

A small chorus of *"Don't like the way, you treat my cat!"* Broke out.

"They must really want to hear Frisky, My Kitty!" Lyn said.

James rolled his eyes. After the kerfluffle on the

Epic, Lyn's song "Frisky" had gotten airplay on intergalactic streams targeted to pet lovers, zoologists, and animal advocates from every backwater rescue camp across the known universe. "Crap," James said. "We've become a novelty act with pet nerds. Just what we needed."

"Who would think a group of animal doctors would be so rowdy," Lyn added.

"Goddammit, Lyn," James cried, holding up his guitar again—a starburst pattern Generation Flyer. The jagged scratch ran across the entire backside. "Will you look at what your cat did to my guitar?"

"So?" Lyn's outfit pulsed as he pushed a shock of his blond hair from his eyes.

"What do you mean, *so?*"

"It's got a scratch in it. Who cares?"

"You call that a *scratch?* It's at least ten centimeters long! That's a *gouge* if there ever was one!"

"Play it up, then," Lyn said, simplifying things like he always did when he didn't want to deal with them. "Put a patch on it. Or paint a logo that points to it. You know, give it some real character. This Machine Hates Cats."

"Are you kidding me? Give it a logo?"

"This Machine Kills Mice." Lyn snickered.

"Screw you," James replied. "You wouldn't say that if it was Victoria we were talking about."

Lyn had named his guitar Victoria. The two were close.

Right now, Victoria was cradled absently in his brother's hands.

"Yes, but we're not talking about Vicky, now, are we?" Lyn said.

James pressed his lips together and glanced back to the crowd.

This was no time to get into it with Lyn.

Again.

They were here because Lyn's hijinks on their maiden tour with the cruise lines had resulted in the arrest of a pair of agents from a crime syndicate who had been operating on the GCL ship *Galactic Epic*. GCL bigwigs, concerned that news about having a galactic crime ring using their ships as business conduits might result in a PR hit, commanded that the Moore Brothers—playing now under their old moniker of The Intergalactic Band of Brilliance—be turned into heroes.

It was as good of PR as any, James assumed.

Focus on the positive and sweep the real story under the gravity well.

Rather than keep them on *Epic*, the butthurt entertainment director of that ship had sloughed them off onto this tour. And even though the ED on *Marvel* wasn't any more excited about the Moore brothers, when "Frisky" hit big, it seemed only natural that they would play the *International Vet of the Year* cruise. Facing that kind of pressure from the GCL board of directors, she hadn't stood a chance of keeping them off the bill.

James didn't care.

Playing *Marvel* was as embarrassing as the other, but at least it paid the bills and if Lyn was right, the extra attention could result in future fortunes.

Who cared if it all felt like a Ponzi scheme?

That's what everything about life as an entertainer

seemed to consist of: pinky-swear promises of payment and future hopes for great gigs in the depths of deep space.

All that mattered now, though, was that the GCL brass had rewarded James and Lyn by booking them as headliners on this jaunt, a decision that had been made over the *Marvel* Entertainment Director's wishes, but one they took on anyway.

Despite the energy in the audience, James was still feeling more than a little put off by the whole thing. All he could think of were all the snippets of songs he'd be able to flesh out if they were in a studio rather than galivanting on a cruise liner.

"Great crowd, eh?" Lyn said, eyes glistening with excitement.

"If only it was all about us," James grumbled, still pissed at Frisky's handiwork.

"Don't be such a Dudley Downer."

"They don't care about us, brother. They're just a bunch of dog doctors here to dance, party, and bolt down enough hard booze and dazzledust that they can forget that they spend their entire lives poking and prodding animals."

"And a good time was had by all!" Lyn called.

James grimaced.

His twin was an adrenaline junkie. Just sitting in the green room backstage, Lyn had gotten amped the moment applause for the opening act crashed over him.

On stage, the emcee was already entering the standard chatter he used to introduce acts.

"Given this is the vets' cruise, I bet I can find

someone to do it," James said, intently scanning the crowd now himself.

"Do what?"

"Kill the cat," he said wistfully.

"No vet is going to euthanize a perfectly healthy cat," Lyn replied.

"Everyone has their price."

James gazed around the crowd, imagining just such an everyone out there among the sea of veterinarians.

"All it would take is enough cash, and a suit of body armor thick enough to let the hitman live to tell after getting inside the range of Frisky's talons."

He sensed the cold countenance of Frisky's presence somewhere in the area but was unable to make out the cat. It was an eerie sensation, a feeling like he was being both watched and judged but unable to figure out from where.

To be fair, James usually liked cats.

And Frisky had a certain *savoir-faire* about him that was attractive in that dangerous kind of way certain cats have. But there was an edge to this cat that James hadn't quite come to grips with. They had only been rooming Frisky for a few weeks, but already James had learned to be wary of the thing. This morning, for example, Frisky had bitten his ankle and then chased him hard enough to make him jump on the bed to get away.

There was no time for the rest of their conversation, though.

Lady types! Gentlecreatures! And all other types of beings known to sentientkind! Please help me welcome—straight off

*their ringing engagement at the Happiest Place in Space —
the Intergalactic Band of Brilliance!!!*

The crowd gave a huge roar.

"This isn't over," James yelled as they ran onto the stage.

"It never is, brother," Lyn called over his shoulder, smiling so broadly that James couldn't tell if Lyn put it on just for him or if his brother was just playing to the audience.

Probably both.

Not that it mattered.

A moment later, taking the requisite pose, Lyn toggled the remote mic. "Good evening, my pretties! Here's something we wrote just for you! I hope you like our newest hit. It's called 'The Intergalactic Vet of the Year!'"

Then they both ripped into the opening strains of their newest song.

This thing is over, what's done is done
After this year he can finally say he won
Give Fido flea bomb, help Fido walk
He'll blow your mind when you hear Fido talk

It's time —It's now —It's here
The time is here for the Vet of the Year

Let's go crazy like in '99
My little red corvette will get us there in time
Lost in the darkness then found a pearl
I'm gonna search for all the magic in the world

It's time –It's now –It's here
The time is here for the Vet of the Year
It's time –It's now –It's here
The time is here for the Party of the Year

This thing is over, he won at last
We thought his sorry ass would fade into the past
So grab your partner, grab your friend
We're going to planet Zorb, it's right around the bend

It's time –It's now –It's here
The time is here for the Vet of the Year
It's time –It's now –It's here
The time is here for the Party of the Year

There's Captain Kirk, propped up and posin'
Official mascot of the cryogenically frozen
Hey, there's Jeff Lynne (hey there's Jeff Lynne)
he's drinking gin
He looks so happy must have cloned himself again

It's time –It's now –It's here
The time is here for the Vet of the Year
It's time –It's now –It's here
The time is here for the Party of the Year

CHAPTER 2

igh in the rafters where his Maltese fur helped him blend into the shadows, Frisky the cat sat on a thin pipe that ran across the stage. He had hunched down to keep his profile low and had opened his eyes wide to keenly study the lighting bots that were running back and forth on their tracks to keep spotlights on the performers.

Frisky observed cautiously as the bots flipped beams of light from purple to gold to scintillating rainbows. The brothers' song rolled along, though why anyone cared was beyond him. There were so many other things to pay attention to, after all.

Fascinating, the cat thought as the nearest bot zigged and zagged, twittering and clattering with mechanical precision.

He pondered why the bots were not pointing their lights at a cat.

This made no sense. If there was a cat in the room, it should be the center of all attention. And, given the theme of this cruise, there *were* most definitely cats in the room.

Several, actually.

Not that he cared for them beyond noting the normal sense of social hierarchy that was being so rudely and so typically ignored.

Of course, this was a two-way horror for his feline sensibility.

While cats *deserved* such attention, as a rule, they did not *want* it.

Not often, anyway.

Except when they did.

And except that such attention *should* be provided, of course. And except to note that the lack thereof required meting out proper punishments of scratching and biting.

This was the dichotomy that came with being a cat, though.

He did not mind such weighty dissonances.

Luckily, the service bots drew Frisky's attention.

Service robots were *not* tasty, but they *were* fun to play with.

If nothing else, pouncing on them helped hone his sense of timing—and it was always exciting later when he could watch the crew try to figure out what had happened to their toys as they tried to put them back together again.

One of the devices drew closer.

Frisky's claws ached for action.

His tail twitched.

Below, the boys were playing their ridiculous instruments and strutting around like they were something to pay attention to. They were okay, Frisky supposed. Loud and bothersome at times, but better than the idiot he'd been with before them. At least Lyn and James were both voice-tied to the food generator, and both knew how to work it. Since there were two of them, it was also easy to dupe them into feeding him twice. Frisky liked his meats.

And he liked playing with their instruments when they weren't around, too, except when they fell over and made that horrible clatter the brothers called music.

But mostly Frisky liked that neither was particularly diligent with the doors when they left the cabin. It meant it wasn't hard for a motivated cat to slip out whenever the mood hit.

And, if nothing else, Frisky was always a motivated cat.

The closest bot whined nearby as it flashed a twisting purple beam toward the stage. Below, the boys' sounds were just as loud and obnoxious as any other time they played.

Frisky waited while the bot dodged first one way, then the next, until ... finally ... it was nearby.

He flew across the mechanical rafters, then leaped up to crash into the metallic body.

The tiny bot flipped over onto its tiny back and gave a deliciously satisfying squeal as its lifters broke from the trail it was following and its case clattered against the flat plane of the rail it had been traversing.

Rolling uncontrollably, the bot's purple light suddenly flashed in Frisky's face.

Ack!

He was blind!

Seeing nothing but glowing red globs, unable to help himself, and with reflexes like the cat he was, Frisky jumped away.

His front paws hit what might have been a bot rail.

Then slipped.

Crap.

He was tumbling then, yowling, and twisting, and ducking one shoulder down like he knew how to do, tucking and turning his backside around, sweeping his tail forward then back to get himself under control, but still falling through open air toward the stage below.

A twist of the head and he was at least oriented properly.

His eyesight partially returned as he extended his claws, bracing his legs for impact. Glancing down, he saw he was going to land …

right …

on …

James's …

shoulder.

Excellent!

A moment later, he brought his descent to an abrupt halt by sinking his claw into James's flesh. The landing was perfect. His claws sunk in deeply, and the sound of ripping fabric from James's outfit let everyone know he was fine.

Between song beats though, James gave a sharp scream.

Lyn kept playing as, in one motion, Frisky retracted his claws and used the momentum from his arrested tumble to roll away, landing in perfect control back on the stage.

A moment later, Lyn, too, stopped playing.

The audience sat stunned.

"Mrrroww," Frisky called as he shook his fur out, stretched, and then, standing taller and with eyes bright, sat down and gazed around at the stage.

Well, he thought, *that was fun.*

The audience broke out in unrestrained laughter.

"What the hell?" James said, finally focusing on the cat as he stood whimpering and cradling his shoulder, trying to staunch the blood that was just now beginning to well up.

"Meet our little kitty!" Lyn called to the audience, motioning toward Frisky as the laughter subsided. "He's a bit of a monster, but at least he's *our* monster!"

"Meow," Frisky called again.

More laughter.

"Now I *am* going to kill you!" James cried.

Finally in control of his senses again, James grabbed his guitar by the neck and swung it as if it was a hammer of the gods and he was preparing to bean the cat.

Frisky remained impassive.

Try me, he thought. *Just try me.*

He raised one paw with a single talon unsheathed. The talon point caught the light.

Now the laughter was deafening.

"*Go on!*" someone yelled encouragement to Frisky. "*Bite him!*"

"*Claw him!*"

"*Scratch his eyes out!*"

Frisky flicked his ear, his equivalent of rolling his eyes.

They thought it was part of an act! People are so stupid.

"Come on now, James!" Lyn said, catching his brother's swinging guitar in mid-swoop. "We can't be killing the cat here among all these veterinarians!"

"Just watch me!" James ripped the instrument from Lyn's hand as the crowd broke into unconstrained laughter. The only thing that saved Frisky this time was that James's shoulder gave out while he raised the guitar. The crowd calmed only a little.

That's one nice looking scratch, Frisky thought as he took in his earlier handiwork on James's guitar. *But it needs another to get the full aesthetic.*

Plans filled his head.

Lyn jumped into the moment.

"Sorry to report that killing the cat's not happening tonight, James. But you know what we *can,* do, right?"

"What's that?"

"We can play these good people our favorite cat song! They practically requested it!"

Lyn took a pose and let a chord ring out.

Bite me!
Scratch me!
Claw me!
Frisky!

T he crowd laughed again.

    "Veterinarians from around the universe," Lyn said. "I hope you enjoy this rendition of *Frisky!*"

    Reluctantly, and with great care, James shouldered his instrument and took his part.

Aw Frisky, tear my eyeballs out, scratch the hell out of me,
Frisky
Aw Frisky, why don't you scratch my throat, spill my blood
onto my coat

I don't like the way you treat my cat
You better get out of here you dirty rat
Well I'm sorry he scratched you on the ball
But you shouldn't run naked down the hall

Frisky my kitty, hurt my buddy, Frisky
Frisky my kitty, hurt my buddy, Frisky

My cat's not nasty he's rather nice
Except maybe for a couple of mice
Ya he might have a temper and get out of line
But truth be told he's a damn fine feline

. . .

Well I don't like the way that you treat my cat
You better get out of here you dirty rat
Well I'm sorry he scratched you on the ball
But you shouldn't run naked down the hall

Frisky my kitty, hurt my buddy, Frisky
Frisky my kitty, hurt my buddy, Frisky

Unimpressed, Frisky sauntered off the stage, taking a swipe at the curtain system on the way out.

The crowd went wild.

CHAPTER 3

A wall of applause followed the Intergalactic Band of Brilliance into the dressing room.

It was a small chamber, but comfortable enough. A thin, but constantly refreshed buffet spread lined one wall, smelling of condiments and the Vendergrass cinnamon Lyn had put into the contract simply to see if anyone scanned it. Each corner was embedded with comfortable zero-g furniture pods, stylishly complemented with attached tables of sleek chrome and hard atomic fiber. The walls held slowly shifting images of musicians and actors who had performed on *Marvel*'s stage.

"Hey," Lyn said as they stepped in. "Isn't that the Feral Sisters?"

But the image was gone before James had a chance to look.

He fell into a pod and twisted his shoulder around so he could see his wound better. The shirt was ripped and blood-soaked. He dabbed at his claw marks which, though unhappily deep, would eventually heal.

The shirt was done for, though.

It glistened with crimson seepage.

"I'm going to have to go to Sick Bay and get a rabies shot," he said. "Do you know how painful those things are?"

Lyn, still pumped from the stage, laughed. "Don't be such a diva. It's just a scratch. Besides, we eradicated rabies years ago."

"Who knows where that cat's claws have been?"

Frisky stepped into the green room, hopped deftly onto the buffet table, and helped himself to the pâté.

"Wasn't he great out there!" Lyn said, risking life and limb to scratch the cat on his crown.

James watched the cat devour the food—without attacking Lyn's fingers.

Asshole.

Frisky had returned to the stage while they finished the show, causing no end of comic relief, which just served to piss James off even more.

"We're supposed to be serious musicians. Not a comedy act."

"Lighten up, man. Frisky is worth his weight in gold."

"Yeah," James said. "Maybe if I weren't so drained of blood, I'd…"

"You'd what?" a voice came from the doorway, which had slid silently open.

It was a tall man of startling countenance, so slim James figured he had grown up in one of the hundreds of low-g environments in the known universe. He wore a russet suit, quite modern in its style, business casual with pressure pads stitched up the front and the collar turned properly chic—one side up, the other down—to reveal a second black undertone. The man's skin was dark and smooth, youthful in appearance, leaning toward a blue tint that said he was an outworlder. His hair was carrot top red. He glided forward on a dashing set of antigravity shoes, then stopped before them with a snap of electricity that dropped him gently to the floor.

It was a countenance that James admitted was hard not to pay attention to.

The stranger was handsome in a completely androgynous fashion.

As he settled into the room, a stench that James could only call *formaldehyde* wafted in with him.

It came from an assistant of some kind, who followed the man in. He was younger than the first man, and quite a bit smaller, balancing a glowing recorder on a short stick and edging to one side to get a good angle. Once the assistant fully entered the room, James saw the youth was a Tallian, a race that came from the Stallys Six system and that was occasionally mistaken for a Terran until one got close enough to note their slitted irises and their seven fingers.

This one was dressed in enough sleek black to create an artsy aura so strong as to suggest he came from a long line of pretension and wasn't afraid to admit it.

Old school, James realized.

The most pretentious of the pretentious. He'd run into them before—creatives who clung to the older, better ways. That godawful chemical smell came from hours and hours locked in an enclosed room processing his visuals.

"May I introduce you to Dr. Args von Waschenkaten," the assistant said.

"I don't think James needs a doctor," Lyn said.

"That's good," the tall man replied. "Because I'm not interested in either you or your brother."

"Then who are you—" James paused, then followed the doctor's gaze to where Frisky was now licking his chops.

"Ah," Lyn said. "You're a veterinarian."

"Not just a veterinarian," the assistant said in a voice taken aback. "Dr. von Waschenkaten is the honorary Intergalactic Veterinarian of the Year Cruise's Intergalactic Veterinarian of the Year!"

"I see," Lyn said.

"Redundant much?" James added.

"Mraow," Frisky said, flicking his tail in the ultimate pile-on.

"Dr. von Waschenkaten is the reason this cruise exists!"

The vet raised a sparkling monocle to one widened eye, which was a gemlike green, then bent at the waist to peer at the cat. Frisky's dark eyes blinked with intense boredom. The monocle lens telescoped out to give the vet a magnified view.

Still unimpressed, Frisky simply sat upright with a curious expression on his gaze. Finally, one whisker tweaked, and he licked his chops before giving a single, low growl.

"I see," von Waschenkaten said in a whisper.

Rising to his full height, he slipped the monocle into his pocket.

"You're a bit obnoxious, aren't you, my little friend."

Frisky flipped a solid tail again.

James gripped his guitar tighter. The good doctor was skating his antigrav shoes right up to the line. "I'd be careful if I were you. Frisky has only two settings: begrudging tolerance, and bloodletting."

"Quite the resistant one, too, I see," von Waschenkaten continued, ignoring James's warning. He stepped left, then right, examining Frisky from more angles. "Outstanding," the veterinarian said loudly. "Just outstanding."

"I wouldn't go that far," James replied, cradling his shoulder.

"I'm giving a talk tomorrow at second 1:00 on this same stage you were on. I'll expect you there a half hour early."

"Excuse me?" Lyn said.

"The day is split into two thirteen-hour chunks," replied the veterinarian's assistant. "So, by second one, Dr. V means fourteen hours into the ship's local day."

"We don't need you to teach us how to read a goddamned clock," James snapped.

"A half hour early?" Lyn replied.

"I'll want to prepare the cat properly."

"Prepare the cat?" James replied. "Is that even possible?"

Frisky hissed. Despite all eyes on him, he still managed to scratch Dr. von Waschenkaten on the hand before jumping down and scampering out the doorway.

The veterinarian raised his hand to his mouth and sucked on the torn meaty part. Rather than raising his anger, though, the attack brought a soft, almost beatific sense of admiration to von Waschenkaten's gaze. "Yes, indeed. Outstanding specimen," he said.

"Prepare the cat for what?" Lyn said as the moment returned.

"For the talk, of course," von Waschenkaten replied, standing taller again.

"The talk?"

"Come, come, now, boys. I know you're only musicians, but you're both going to have to keep up better if you're going to be part of history."

"Part of history?" Lyn said.

"You're not instilling confidence," von Waschenkaten replied.

"Hey now!" James replied, finally standing up, his guitar neck firmly gripped in one fist. "You've got a lot of nerve coming in here and throwing insults around like that."

"I beg your pardon?" von Waschenkaten said. "I'm the Intergalactic Vet of the Year."

"I don't care if you're the Intergalactic *Twit* of the Year. I'm the only one who can give Lyn that kind of shit. But here you come, blowing in here like you're some kind of a grand savant and tossing insults around like we're just supposed to take them. *Then* you tell us to be somewhere or be square? You've got to be kidding me."

Sensing the tension permeating the room, the assistant bent the camera low to give the moment a dramatic angle.

The veterinarian stood tall as if simply waiting.

"I'm sorry," von Waschenkaten finally said. "Were

you done? For a moment there, I really did think you were getting someplace with all that."

James lifted his instrument. "I think I ought to use your head to put another gouge in my guitar."

"Let's not be doing anything stupid now," the veterinarian said, waving an open palm.

A moment of silence cloaked the room.

"What is your talk about?" Lyn asked from his corner of the room.

"My talk?"

"Surely you know of Dr. von Waschenkaten's break-through." The assistant's thin voice came as if from outside a distant cloud.

"With all the news of Galactic Peace and the possi-bility of a black hole swallowing the world," James replied, remembering this morning's headlines. "It seems that we missed out on Dr. von Whosisl's little whatever."

"The doctor has a new technology," the assistant replied.

"Shush," von Waschenkaten broke in protectively, heat suddenly giving his cheeks a deeper blue tint. "That's top secret for now. Need to know, only, and no one needs to know until the big reveal."

The assistant blushed in shame for having gone too far.

The veterinarian turned to the brothers.

"Just bring the feline," he said. "I'll need a volunteer, and this one is … um … purrfect!"

James rolled his eyes.

With that, von Waschenkaten turned on his heel and left the brothers' dressing room.

Caught off guard, the assistant mumbled apologies and left a moment later.

"What the hell was that?" Lyn said.

"No clue," James replied. "But I think we've got an appointment. On the bright side, maybe von Wonder-Nuttinbergin will take care of that euthanasia thing for me."

"Stop joking about that. Please."

James glanced at his guitar, then to the doorway Frisky had disappeared through. "Who's joking?"

A moment later, the door slid open again, and a green-skinned support staff wonk stepped efficiently into the dressing room. The logo on her shirt marked her as a show tech. Jib-Madana, James remembered. She was a young stagehand he had talked to earlier in the day.

"The entertainment director would like to see you now," Jib said.

"Can it wait until tomorrow?" Lyn said, blowing an overly fatigued sigh. "I'm bushed."

The tech shrugged. "I can tell her to wait if you want?"

"I want."

"All right." Jib stepped back and the door shut.

"That was kind of cheeky," James said.

Lyn sat back in a pod and bit into a cracker. "I like this Vendergrass cinnamon. It's very tasty."

"You know the director isn't going to take being blown off like that."

"Well. Screw her if she can't take a joke."

James raised his eyebrow.

"We're booked for two weeks and the ship's already left port, brother. What's the worst that can happen?"

"Airlocks," James said, imagining doors closing with them both on the wrong side of the vacuum. "That's the worst that can happen."

Lyn sat up, grabbed a handful of something that might have been ginger snaps from the snack bowl, then popped one into his mouth before sprawling on the couch again.

"Don't be silly, brother. No one is going to toss a headliner out the airlocks."

"Famous last words," James said.

CHAPTER 4

"I can't believe you're dragging me out to that place," Lyn said, wrapping a scarf of rough fabric around his neck and checking himself in the cabin's small mirror.

The *Marvel* was a half hour away from the cruise's first touristy stop at something called the Vast Tanadi Plains—renowned for a collection of wild creatures that certainly qualified as a veterinarian's wet dream. It was a popular excursion, its roster already crammed full when James first inquired about it. But the brothers had gotten special captain's passes because James finally agreed to do a PR run in support of their tour, and the GCL brass swooned.

Lyn sported a newly bought pair of camping pants and a composite tech jacket designed to filter air into a rebreather system (*great for off-world accidents, visits to gas planets, and even SCUBA diving!*). A pair of prismatic-lensed pilot's goggles perched on his forehead made his blond hair ruck up in wild tendrils. Earlier he'd finished packing a box of condensed provisions that should keep them both in eats for weeks.

"You really didn't need to go overboard," James said, peering around his brother to check the mirror. James wore simple safari duds and a two-toned visor. "It's just a tourist thing. No need to go full survivalist on me."

"Yeah, right," Lyn said. "Just a three-hour tour, you say?"

"We'll be back before you know it."

"You never know when you might get stranded."

"Do you know how much that rig cost us?"

Lyn glared at James, as his brother took his full turn at the mirror. "As if you're one to talk."

"All I bought special was that overcoat," James said, not wanting to get into it again.

Lyn had gotten on a fashion kick the past week, and there was nothing to do but let it run its course. With any luck, this phase would pass before Lyn discovered the New Brittny's Jewelry outlet on board the ship. It specialized in Nebula-pressed green diamonds, and if Lyn saw one of those they might be in hock for the rest of their lives.

James couldn't keep himself from glancing across their tiny cabin to admire the overcoat he'd bought for the tour. It was pure fashion. He planned to wear it on stage tonight. His mind flashed on posing for PR photos as they stepped off stage. The idea was a shade more than intoxicating.

"You're the one who got excited about the wildlife on a cruise," James replied, pulling wrinkles out of the overcoat.

"Different kind of wildlife," Lyn snapped.

"Just using your words."

"Don't be a dingle on purpose, brother. It doesn't suit you." Lyn paused. "You only want to do this little tour to make my life hell."

"I want to do this little tour because I saw a cool virtch for it and because it'll be a gas to see the animals. It should also give us a chance to do something to help the brand, you know? Like you're always talking about. That you're annoyed because this wasn't your idea is simply an added benefit." James grinned in the way he did when he was poking at his twin.

Lyn fumed.

"You don't have to come along, you know."

"And leave you alone to do something stupid in front of recorders?"

"That's a hoot coming from you, brother."

Lyn grimaced, then raised his hands over his head. "We're headliners, James! That's the dream, right? Sleep all day, do a big gig, then play all night! All this running around in the daytime is going to cramp our style."

"I thought the dream was to be artists," James said. "You know, make music. Hang out in recording studios checking out the girls. *That* was the dream. Screw the sellouts. We just wanted to make enough cash to do the music we wanted to do."

"That was before we found out how much fun it is to be headliners," Lyn quipped. "We can be artists *after* we're set for life."

James rolled his eyes. "The way you're going through our cash accounts, that's going to be a long way off."

"Right," Lyn said. "So why take the risk of going planetside and getting eaten by a long-horned saber-saurous?"

"There's no such thing. It's a Lagardian tiger."

"As if that makes a difference." Lyn frowned and looked at the system clock. "A safari experience," he scoffed, rolling his eyes with simply the tone of his voice. "We could be lounging by the pool, making our way through the entire menu of drinks, and letting every hot veterinarian on the cruise pick us up."

"We've got our whole lives to do that," James said, turning from the mirror. Outside the portal, the planet drew near. The tour's boarding call was fifteen minutes away.

"Not if we're eaten by a wild zar-vart, we don't."

"We won't be eaten by a wild zar-vart."

"I won't, anyway," Lyn said.

James gave him a deadpan gaze, waiting for whatever was coming.

"I can run faster than you," Lyn explained.

A sharp tone from the intership communications system made both brothers jump.

"What's that?" James said.

The blue flash said the message came on the internal service frequency, so it was a private notice rather than the public service announcement that might have reported it was time to lock down for planetary entry maneuvers.

"Respond," James toggled the device.

This is a message for: Moore, James, and Lyn, the system announced. *Entertainment Elements four and five.*

"Are you element four or am I?" James said to Lyn.

Lyn let his eyes grow wide in silent sarcasm, then adjusted his goggles down over his eyes before giving his brother the thumbs-up.

"Proceed," James gave the formal toggle.

Cruise Entertainment Director Roumie requests your immediate attendance at a session in her office space.

"Please explain to the director that we have a prior engagement," James said smugly.

Lyn giggled.

Neither of the boys had any desire to see the entertainment director.

It turns out that entertainment directors talk, and the woman was no more enthusiastic to have the Moore brothers on board than the director on *Epic* had been before her—meaning not interested at all. She'd made it abundantly clear that they were here only because GCL head honchos had demanded it. But just because she wasn't going to win a battle with the big bosses, didn't mean she couldn't make the brothers' lives a living hell in the process.

The less interaction, the better.

Prior engagement? the system replied.

"Another commitment," Lyn quipped, the prismatic lenses of his goggles making his gaze kaleidoscope. "A plan for the day. A mark on the calendar. A thing we need to—"

"Ahem."

James cleared his throat to quiet his brother, knowing Lyn could go on all day.

Taking the hint, Lyn finished up. "So sorry we can't make it, but we've been looking forward to this excursion for years."

"Please request the director reschedule for tomorrow," James added.

You are informed that your engagement with the Vast Tanadi Plains excursion has been canceled.

"Canceled?"

Revoked, the system replied. *No longer valid. Kaput. Sailed into the West. Dropped into vacuum storage.*

"No need to go overboard," James said, looking daggers at Lyn and sensing a wave of irritation on the artificial intelligence behind the system.

Denied, the system continued. *Squashed. Sent to the deep brine of Negasis Twelve.*

"All right, we heard you," James exclaimed.

The conversation hit a lull.

James's stomach fell with the realization that they weren't going anywhere today. "So we're stuck on this cruise, and now we can't even take advantage of it."

Lyn pushed his goggles up. His grimace of solace was not convincing.

Can I report to the Cruise Entertainment Director that you will be attending now?

The brothers exchanged glances.

Lyn shrugged. "Doesn't sound like we have much of a choice."

"All right," James said to the system, "let the director know we'll be on our way in a moment."

The connection rang off.

"You don't have to look so relieved, brother," James said.

He could hear Lyn's comment without asking for it.

For Lyn, a thirty-minute conversation with a bloviating entertainment director was worth the price of missing the safari tour.

T en minutes later, the director's office door irised open and the brothers entered.

"You called, Boss Lady?" Lyn quipped.

"Hello, Director," James said. "We were on our way planetside. What's so wrong it couldn't have waited?"

"Both of yas, sit down," Asa Roumie, the director, said. She was a human by birth but had been in space with the cruise lines for longer than Lyn and James had been alive. The deep rasp of her voice conflicted with the slight nature of her frame. She waved a bony hand at a set of dingy artificial gravity chairs across from the sweeping expanse of her desk. The brothers moved to take their positions.

The director was a tall, whip-thin woman with a voice that was thick from some kind of accident that neither of the brothers was interested in enough to ask about. One rumor tossed around the entertainment deck said she'd swallowed bad water on a remote planet. Others said a lover kicked her when they found out she'd been cheating on them. The identity of that lover changed with every telling. Either way, GCL *Marvel*'s Entertainment Director Asa Roumie was a friend of GCL *Epic*'s entertainment director, which, given the hijinks that had occurred on the *Epic* cruise, was not good news for the boys in the band. He had made his distaste for the brothers well enough known to Roumie that James didn't want to get into a lengthy conversation about it.

Her green and gray Galactic Cruise Lines jumpsuit was as wrinkled as her forehead, and the perfume she'd drenched herself in made it seem like she hadn't showered since well before launch.

The remains of three days of lunches were piled up on the far edge of her desk—mostly packets of wilted celery and crusty remnants of what might have been ranch dressing. Several layers of control screens glowed in mid-air at places around the cabin, their colors flashing in weirdly synchronous patterns. She waved them away and leaned forward to focus her sharp, violet gaze on the brothers.

"I understand Dr. von Waschenkaten was in to talk to you earlier."

"Yes, indeed. It was a pleasure to meet good old kitty washer," Lyn quipped.

"And that you implied your cat wasn't going to help him," Roumie continued, ignoring Lyn's insolence.

"Well, it's not like we have much say in the matter," James said.

"It's your cat, idn't it?"

"Well," Lyn said, eyebrows raised. "Um …"

"The key word there is *cat*, ma'am," James said, jumping in to save his brother from saying whatever stupid thing he had been ready to say. "There's only so much we can make Frisky do."

He gave his still-healing shoulder an involuntary roll, and his gut churned as he recalled the gouge in his guitar. Frisky's opening night adventures were still fresh, too.

The director waved a dismissive hand.

"Lock it," she said. "I don't want to hear any more of that kind of thing."

"Ma'am?" Lyn said.

"It's a *cat*, right?"

"Frisky?"

"Of course, Frisky, you dolt. Who the hell else would I be calling a cat?"

"Well, you could have meant my brother who is a silly cat. Or you could have been talking about me, who is a cool cat—"

The director looked at James. "If you don't want to be immediately terminated for your insubordination, I suggest you shut him up."

"Yes, ma'am," James replied, giving an admonishing glare that brought Lyn to silence.

He chewed his lip for a moment, then replied.

"The cat is a, um, yes. Frisky is a cat."

"And?" The entertainment director peered dramatically at the boys, leaned forward, and tilted her head to make her violet-eyed gaze feel even more laserlike. "You two are the *humans*, right?"

"Yes, but—"

"Do you understand what a big deal Dr. von Waschenkaten is on this ship? Do you understand how hard I had to work to make sure the dolt of a doctor would come here? Do you understand what it means to wine and dine a man like that for weeks to ensure his booking? To…" She shut her mouth, then shuddered. Images of von Washercat and the entertainment director went through James's mind. Next thing, he was shuddering too.

There were things about the entertainment industry better left unsaid.

Lyn replied before James could.

"Of course, we know Dr. Water Stashen Vashen is a big deal," Lyn said, sarcasm dripping from each syllable. "He's the Intergalactic Veterinarian of the Year!"

The director opened her mouth, then closed it again, staring plasma bolts in Lyn's direction.

"Please shut up," James finally said.

At least Lyn had the common decency to cower at that.

"Well, they did name the whole cruise after him, didn't they?" Lyn said meekly.

"The whole cruise is on this ship because *I* brought von Waschenkaten here," Roumie said, seething. A lock of her frosted hair fell waywardly over one eye. "I will not have the entire setup ripped apart by two no-name minstrels."

"Hey, there," Lyn said.

"Lyn!" James called.

"We've got names," Lyn said meekly as he sank into his chair again. "We're the Intergalactic Band of Brilliance."

A moment of silence followed, broken only by the sound of the director's forced air fan unit kicking on. The air grew fresher for that moment. Alas, it could not last.

"I should fire you now," the entertainment director said.

James read the longing on her face, accompanied by the pain of the constraints she had to be feeling from the GCL brass, and came to a new conclusion.

Yes, he thought.

They had some power here, too.

"All right, Director," James said, leaning forward and turning the tables. "We both know you can't chuck us out right here and right now or you'd already have done it. You need us to play our gigs. We need you to stay out of our hair. So how about we stop all this posturing and cut to the chase? What do you want us to do?"

Roumie gave an unhappy grimace. Her fingertips drummed hard on her desk.

"Yeah. As fun as it would be, I can't fire you unless you become directly insubordinate."

"So, tell us what you need," James said. "And we'll see what we can do."

"Dr. von Waschenkaten's public presentation is part of our programming. Which means it falls under my control."

"And that means if we screw him up, you'll be within your rights to have your way with us," James said.

"Exactly." Roumie's smile was so sharp it stabbed. "It also means that if von Waschenkaten wants the cat at his little shindig, I need the cat at his little shindig."

The twins sat back in tandem. Lyn shrugged in resignation.

"All right, then," James said. "We'll do it."

"So Frisky *will* show up for Dr. von Waschenkaten's talk?"

"Exactly," James replied, pushing his hand on Lyn's forearm when his brother was going to speak.

"Or you *will* be fired," Roumie finished. "Do we have an understanding?"

"It's all good by me," James said.

"Um … sure," Lyn added with a tone of voice that James understood meant his brother meant no such thing. One problem at a time, though.

"Good," the entertainment director said with an overly dramatic flourish. "Now get out of here before the sight of you makes me puke."

CHAPTER 5

It was thirty minutes before Dr. von Waschenkaten's talk, and already the auditorium hall was cram packed. Body heat warmed the air, and the acoustics of the open theater were not robust enough to fully absorb the steady rumble of voices. There had been buzz about the presentation all day. He was rumored to be ready to make a major announcement of some sort, which meant this was the year's inside event of inside events for all the veterinarians here.

Feeling an artificial sense of confidence, Secret Agent Mann scoffed as he accepted his napkin-wrapped container of Lasarian chardonnay from the open bar dispensary at the back of the hall. The announcement was probably a new Zorbian rectal thermometer, or something equally as impactful.

Turnout was strong, though.

He turned away from the dispenser and scratched the side of his cheek, then his biceps.

Then his thigh.

The entire collection of veterinarians was covered with dander from some exotic animal now. He'd piped in antihistamine boosters before coming. Now he had to stop thinking about it to keep the placebo effect from triggering his allergies again.

He gave a huge sneeze, drawing attention and nearly resulting in spilling the wine.

Damnation.

"Pardon me," Mann muttered too sharply as he carefully protected his drink and stepped past a pod gathering of five veterinarians standing nearby.

His sensors had picked up their energetic conversation earlier, about the creation of avatar services across galaxies.

"It's coming, my friends!" one already sloshed vet said to the collective in a voice that was too loud even in the din of the assembly. "You must get into this on the front wave!"

"I read a report that the first doctor who tried it killed fifteen beloved pets before they got shut down."

"Never mind that!" the first replied. "It's progress! And progress is inevitable! If you're not on this now, you'll be left behind for certain."

Mann puffed his chest as he slipped past. "It's sure to be a winner with the financial markets," he said with a glint in his eye he was particularly fond of, then went on to edge farther toward his seat.

"Indeed!" the drunk veterinarian called out after him, but Secret Agent Mann was already far enough away that he could disengage.

He smirked, though.

The best idiots are the ones that never know they're on the butt end of jokes.

Financial markets loved schemes like this, and these veterinarians were going to be fresh meat on the counter for them. He scratched the hives on his biological shoulder, and forcibly refrained from scoffing further at the veneer of social importance that oozed from the crowded collective.

He had chosen Tag Nole for his personality this evening specifically because the dude was a cool cat. Nole was one of his favorite characters. His *Q-Space* stories were always exciting, and Mann had always liked the debonair vibe Nole could achieve whenever it was needed. Since von Waschenkaten's talk felt chock-full of hoity-toitiness, and since Mann was trying to pass as a veterinarian, this event seemed to be a perfect time for Tag Nole, Undercover.

The upside to his choice was that, in his most business casual jumpsuit and cradling his container of Lasarian chardonnay in the same way Nole did in *Q-Space Gambler*, Secret Agent Mann fit into the gathering well enough. This was unusual for him. While the metallic skin of his face and left side were flexible and fully configured to match human appearance, they tended to draw attention.

And Mann did not like attention.

Both for the obvious fact that he was a secret agent, and attention as a secret agent was a bad thing, and because he had never been good with people anyway.

Left to his own devices he didn't know when to talk and when not to talk. And, when he *did* decide to contribute, he often found himself sharing too much or going off-topic so far that his conversational partners would grow zombified with boredom.

It was all very embarrassing.

Which, of course, was why—whenever he found himself in a situation where he needed to address people for any time whatsoever—he found it more comfortable to tie into the massive databanks of speeches and video shows he had access to, find a character that seemed appropriate at the time, and jack into their personality file to mimic their style.

If nothing else, putting on someone cooler than him made him feel more confident.

In general, though, he preferred to stay in the background and let his optical and radio wave sensors do their thing. Much easier that way. Better for everyone involved, really.

Tonight, though, among veterinarians from all walks of the galaxy, Secret Agent Mann did not stand out as particularly noteworthy, and his choice of Tag Nole helped him blend into the world around him just fine.

The downside of his selection, however, was that it came with an almost intense air of disrespect for anything that reeked of ostentation.

Tag Nole was the common man's agent. He played hard and he played fair. He enjoyed his women and his men, and he always came out on top, often after dropping the bad guy with a solid one-two combination and a roundhouse uppercut. That last part wasn't going to come into play here, but once Mann had plugged into Nole's *Q-Space* persona there was no getting around his basic personality. And, while Nole himself could compartmentalize well enough to hide his disrespect, a carried persona could go only so far.

Secret Agent Gustave Mann was still a work in process.

Still, he managed to avoid confrontation until he arrived at his assigned seat, a single billet in the back row of the moderately sized presentation pod.

As he sat down the seat's safety system buzzed, and a soft voice came to him.

In the unlikely event the assembly hall loses pressure and power to the ship's antigravity systems, we recommend enacting the automatic seat constraints built into your pod.

Mann grumbled and balanced his drink on the armrest as he settled in.

All he wanted to do was pay attention to the crowd.

At least one of them was likely a crook. Maybe more. His job was to figure out which one, and exactly what they were doing. Normally he would avoid a social setting like this, but it seemed a great time to watch the collective play. All his sensors were engaged. He was looking for behavior out of the ordinary. Unfortunately, it turned out, veterinarians on a cruise did nothing but behave in ways that were out of the ordinary.

He ignored the warning and sipped the wine.

It wasn't like any chardonnay he'd ever had before. Dark, rather than light. Syrupy rather than dry and oaky. He wasn't sure he liked it. He should have ordered a simple Florox martini with a twist, which would have been better. But Tag Nole drank Lasarian chardonnay in *Dropdown City*, so Lasarian chardonnay it was.

Normally he didn't drink on the job, but he had to fit in, right?

The sip brought the bite of the liquor back. It was growing on him.

The gathering of veterinarians was subdued now, most standing in the raised sections that ringed the auditorium, tipping cocktails and sniffing one of the many complimentary intellect boosters the cruise lines made available 26/7. He set his passive sensors to gather information in a steady stream—which meant more work later but ensured he could take his time analyzing the veterinarians one at a time for now.

Taking them in manually, though, Mann felt a distinct *here to be seen* flavor to the collective, noting eyes that danced from attendee to attendee and wandering optical tentacles that constantly surveilled the crowd.

He'd already gone through the records of every veterinarian on the ship's roster, though, digging deep and looking for every sign of a fake persona he could.

He'd come up with bupkis.

Every vet aboard had fully certified documentation. Sure, *those* could be faked, too, but he'd piped the entire database through the Q-deck interface and used the mega-burst optical computational systems back at the Galactic Investigation Bureau. He'd sliced and diced the logs, scoured through a hundred different security mechanisms, and even tried physical observation.

Even they couldn't give him better directions than "keep your eyes out."

Thanks for that, buddies. Careful or you'll shoot yer eye out.

Several of the veterinarians had spent the day galivanting over the planet's infamous safari tour, so they were tired—which accounted for the hush that lay over the crowd. The attendees had dressed for the event, all in pressed suits and layered dresses. The Denebian across the way flaunted a poncho-like drape that obscured enough of their bruise-colored shape that it was almost easy to look at.

In total, the gathering carried the same intimate but distant aura of anticipation that might come from a top-ranked play or from being in an elite art gallery on the opening night of a new showing.

He scratched the hive on his forearm again, then another on his thigh.

Allergies sucked. Safety warnings sucked.

Unable to stop himself now, he scoffed.

Really?

Veterinarians, gathering and chattering so solemnly about … what?

As if these animal doctors thought they were professionals or something.

They worked on dogs, for criminy sake. How hard could it be? Hand the beast a shoe to chew up and a bone to eat and you're done. Sure, vets went to school just like real doctors. And, sure, veterinarian medicine had gotten more complicated after the galactic trade routes opened and disease transfer rates spiked. Stellar hospital stations and all that. But ever since he'd been a boy and a slobbering beast of a dog had bit him on the behind, he'd known he did not like animals. Why anyone would want to be an animal doctor was beyond him.

Secret Agent Mann blinked his eyes to shut down that line of thought.

Wow.

He really needed to rethink using Tag Nole in this kind of situation.

While he agreed with Nole's basic premise, to show that kind of outward disdain could blow his cover.

As he grumbled, a female Zendak took a seat in the row ahead of him (though with Zendaks, gender was both difficult to determine and, to be fair, quite fluid). She was beautiful, though. Hair dark. Frame strong, but thin. Quite young for a veterinarian. "Did you see the latest in genetic snake swapping?" she said to the half-sotted human beside her. The phrase came with a layer of earnestness thick enough that Mann could feel her nose rising to obscure her view.

"No, I haven't," replied her conversation partner.

The man carried a leering smile that said he had dalliance on his mind as he pressed his hand on her shoulder and leaned toward her ear.

"It sounds utterly fascinating, though. Do tell on."

"The Galactic Association of Specialized Bio-Assisted Genetics says they've created a new form of a lizard."

"A new form of lizard?"

"Yes." The woman took a sip of her cocktail. "Part Gila monster, part deep-sea shrimp."

"Sounds tasty."

"It's not for eating."

"Not for you, maybe." The man wriggled his eyebrows and bounced his head sideways and back.

"Humans are disgusting."

The man, obviously now something past the edge of drunk himself, peered deeply into the Zendak's eyes, then lowered his voice to something he thought was fetching. "Well, we will eat *anything*."

"I don't think you'll be eating this any time soon," the woman said, edging away a notch.

"Don't underestimate me." The man closed the gap again.

"Besides being bipedal and the size of a small vehicle, the new lizard is supposed to be sentient."

"That's not what I'm talking about eating," he said.

"I know what you're talking about. You're not eating that, either."

The man grumbled, then dashed down the rest of his drink.

"Is that all you've got?" he said, straightening up. "Gila monster and shrimp?"

"I think it has elements of Roovian toad DNA, too, which are poisonous if you rub their belly."

"I'm not poisonous if you rub my belly," the man, having decided to take a second pass, leered so sharply he couldn't be ignored.

Except, it seemed, by this Zendak.

"I suspect its epigenetics have been harvested from various other animals."

"Like us disgusting humans, right?"

"More like slugs."

"Now that's interesting. When do you expect we'll be able to vote for it?"

Feeling a wave of pure Nole flush through his body, Secret Agent Mann leaned forward and tapped the man on his shoulder.

The man swiveled.

"I do believe the lady has had enough," Mann said.

"What the hell?" the man stammered. "What do you think you're doing?"

"I think I'm watching an idiot crash and burn," Mann said using his best Nole drone. "Which I admit was fun for a while, but has gone stale with remarkable haste. You need to up your game, sir."

The Zendak covered bemusement with the back of her hand.

He sat back and sipped his wine.

"I think you had a real chance, though. The young lady seemed actually into you before you opened up your trap."

The man stammered further, then appeared to be getting up to address Mann more directly.

As he tottered, the lights flashed and the gathering began to make their way to their seats. The man stabilized on his feet, glanced at Mann, then back at the Zendak. He waved his hand. "Ah, fuggedaboudit," he said, then staggered off to find his seat.

"Thank you," the woman said.

"You're welcome," Mann replied.

"I do have a seat open here if you'd like to come down a row?"

Thanks to his Noleness, Mann smiled despite the anxiety that rose inside him. He hated that.

"No, thank you," he said. "I'm sure I'd only bore you, too."

The lights dimmed further. A spotlight flashed to the back of the auditorium, and the main doorways slid open.

Amid audible gasps, the good Dr. Args von Waschenkaten surfed his way down the aisle toward the stage, his gravity boots giving steady spurts of blue electrical sparks as he flew.

CHAPTER 6

Expecting they would need to be ready soon, Lyn commanded the cat cart—with an unhappy Frisky inside. "Come along, now."

The hovering cage, with its barred walls draped in a plain blue sheet, moved smoothly to his side. A heavy *thunk* came from inside as weight crashed against its side. Then Frisky's growl rose, a sound set on Low and Very Dangerous.

Standing beside Lyn, James dabbed at a series of scratches on his forearm where blood refused to stop welling even thirty minutes after Frisky had created them.

"I hate that cat," James said.

"No, you don't," Lyn replied.

"Pardon my rudeness, but you don't get to say what I hate."

Lyn raised his thin eyebrows.

"That thing is murderous," James added.

"To be fair, Frisky was only defending himself. *You*

were the one making *him* do something *he* didn't want to do."

"That's only because *you* wouldn't put him in the box."

Lyn twisted a corner of his lip and shook his head sideways as if to say *duh*. "We only hate what we can't have," he snapped back.

"What is that supposed to mean?"

Rather than answer, Lyn focused on proceedings on the stage.

They stood stage left, as directed.

Lights focused on the galaxy-renowned veterinarian, and the crowd grew attentive as von Waschenkaten landed his boot-powered flight, then strolled to center stage and squared himself to the audience. The vivid blue of his skintight jumpsuit lent him an air of confidence. A series of soft spotlights made his carrot-red hair and beautifully smooth cheekbones pop, and as he stood stoically to attract attention, the glitter of his green eyes mesmerized the gathering.

Even James found himself forgetting to dab at his wounds.

"What's von Wishywashy going to do?" James said.

Again, Lyn ignored him.

The low clatter of the audience shifting in their seats reverberated through the chamber, then, after a dramatic moment, faded to rapt silence.

"My colleagues," von Waschenkaten said, his voice firm and steady, lifting a graceful hand to welcome them all.

The space behind him became a holographic representation of a vast green field. The sun, barely peeking from the horizon, cast fresh, dazzling light on the dew-covered grass. The clear tone of a flute came low and firm.

"I am here to talk about the most amazing advancement in the history of veterinarian science," von Waschenkaten said. "Something that will advance our field in every imaginable way, from diagnostics to the development of procedures and medicines and to the actual process of treating disease and physical discomfort in the animals we all love so much. But something that, I think, is also just the thinnest of crusts on the planet of animal life that we have been exploring for so long. This is really just the beginning."

As he spoke, the sun rose slowly behind him, and the low note of the flute grew louder.

"Once it's settled out, my finding—and the tools that will result from it—will change far more than *our* field. Indeed, it has the possibility of changing everything about the way we see the world so dramatically that it will raise those creatures we see as our pets to become simply new species—no different from a human, or a Denebian or Flagfort from Sirius."

The huge crowd gasped.

"But first," he said with a sharp turn. "To celebrate the moment, I have a little statement in the form of a song—a little celebration of the moment, as it were." His gaze lifted dramatically to the upstairs booth where the sound and lights administrator systems controlled the environment. He raised his arm in a graceful command.

"Maestro?"

The images of a band rose behind him.

An organ player and a pair of guitars. A shaggy-haired drummer sat behind an impressive kit. A moment later, they began to play, and Dr. von Waschenkaten reached out to cradle the old-time microphone that suddenly appeared on a chromium stand before him. He leaned in and began to sing.

I've done so much to win your trust
I've told the truth, I've even lied
I've held your pet like a child
A trick us vets use to connect

At first, the audience wasn't sure what to think, but they smiled at the intimate nature of the lyrics when it came to their profession. Von Waschenkaten was talking to them, and as the tune progressed, they brightened. Their heads and other appendages began to nod in time with the beat.

"What horrible mess is this?" Lyn said. "The drummer's not even playing!"

James shrugged. A pre-event song hadn't been in the run-through. "He's not bad, really."

Lyn's sarcastic cough voiced his disagreement.

I'm like a movie you don't understand
The longer you watch the closer you get to the end

I need a volunteer
I need a heart to help me here
I need a volunteer
Someone to take a chance on me

I made a breakthrough, that's why I'm here
A keynote speaker extraordinaire
I need a subject to appear
Frisky, come here, or you'll be put to sleep.

"A little dramatic, don't you think?" Lyn said as the artificial guitar moved into a brief solo.

James glanced at Frisky. "I could go with it."

The response from the crowd of vets seemed as mixed as the boys'.

I need a volunteer
I need a heart to help me here
I need a volunteer
Someone to take a chance on me
I need a volunteer
I'm about to do something big
I need a volunteer
This is something you won't believe

T he song concluded, and the audience gave warm applause.

"Thank you," von Waschenkaten said with a curtsey and then a bow. "Thank you very much."

The band behind him faded away, as did the microphone stand.

Then the veterinarian turned to James and Lyn.

"Come along, boys," he said, beckoning them with the fingers of one hand. "Let's not keep the world waiting. Bring out the volunteer! It's time to make history."

Lyn moved to join von Waschenkaten, commanding the cart to follow him.

James trailed the cart.

He was fine being on stage, but now the pressure of eyeballs tracking him felt more uncomfortable. As far as he could tell, neither he nor Lyn had any measurable reason for being here. Without a guitar, he felt naked.

They arrived at their pre-assigned marks.

Von Waschenkaten turned to the opposite wing and motioned his assistant to join him.

The still-black-clad assistant complied, accompanied by another platform that hovered with antigravity. This tray also had a cloth covering it, also plain blue, its edges fluttering with its movement. On the tray was a wide metallic bowl sealed with a thin top.

An array of free-motion cameras followed, each trained on different portions of the event.

Von Waschenkaten was getting into the flow now.

He picked a corner of the cover over Frisky's carrier, then whisked it off.

"Gentlecreatures from around the galaxy, I give you the common housecat."

From between the bars, the audience could see Frisky stoically sitting and staring at the veterinarian with eyes slit.

James recognized the expression of murderous intent.

The crowd gave a polite wave of applause.

"You may be asking yourself why you should care about such a mundane little creature as the average, everyday tomcat. What does he have to do with anything?"

Von Waschenkaten strolled languidly around the small tray and lifted the lid from the bowl to reveal a pile of powder colored such a pale pink that it might as well have been white.

"Jazz dust?" James said out loud too quickly to stop himself.

He didn't use the drug, but he'd seen it more often than he could count. He *was* a musician. Even if the stuff was banned in half the galaxy, he was well aware of its sources.

The site of it made him angry.

All this for a gram of something I could cop anywhere?

"Ha-ha!" the veterinarian cried. "Some might wish that it was that notorious dust of jazz, but no, my little fledgling celebrity music brother, this is so much more valuable than a simple hallucinogen."

The cat growled at the vet's insult.

Frisky tweaked a whisker, lifted a front paw, then bared a claw and bit it as if to sharpen its point.

James did a doubletake, impressed that the cat was coming to his defense.

The veterinarian played to the moment. "Now, now, little kitty, let's have none of that."

The crowd rumbled with something that was half laughter, and half anticipation.

"No, my friends, what we have in this bowl is the newest synthetic neurolizing agent. It's a collection of proprietary enzymes, proteins, and machine learning programs imprinted into a single custom atomic structure—an atomic structure purr-fectly designed to slip through mucous barriers of the body."

"This, my esteemed colleagues and compatriots, is a little something I call Smart Dust!" He lifted a small spoon from beside the bowl, then held it up to the light.

The collective of the galaxy's best veterinarians moved to the edges of their seats.

"And what does this material do, you might ask? Well, let's find out, shall we?"

With his audience enthralled, von Waschenkaten stepped carefully to the cat carrier, and with a single puff, blew the powder directly into the cat's face.

Frisky coughed and spit. His back arched, and a meowing commenced with such drama that once again the crowd laughed despite itself.

The cat kept coughing, though, shaking his head as if to break a bad vision.

His eyes blinked non-stop, and his body lowered to a lounging sphinx position.

His stomach spasmed and his whiskers twitched this way and that.

"What are you doing?" Lyn called, stepping toward

von Waschenkaten with a fist clenched until James stepped in the way.

"Don't do something you'll regret later, brother."

"Oh, I don't intend to regret this!" Lyn replied.

Frisky coughed, then sneezed, then coughed again.

A voice in the audience gasped.

Another called out: "Are you killing that cat?"

"Help him!" another yelled.

Yet von Waschenkaten simply held his hand up, directing them all to pause.

The situation settled and Frisky seemed to get control of himself again.

He stood up on all fours, gray tail winding around his body, then flicking hard against the bars that closed him in.

"You talentless idiot!" Frisky said out loud. "When I get outta this joint, I'm gonna scratch your eyeballs out."

The audience gasped.

Did the cat just talk?

"Yeah, you heard me, Bozo," Frisky said as the veterinarian took a step back. "Your time in this world is heading to zero."

Yes, the cat had talked!

Frisky crashed hard against the bars.

"Holy hairballs, but I hate you vets."

Bedlam broke out. Hands went to heads. Some stood and peered closer, others sat wide-eyed, muttering "what the hell?"

A skinny Denebian laughed so hard it excreted something so caustic that it made three fellow veterinarians make mad dashes to get away from it.

The entire auditorium was now officially bonkers.

Lyn, his cheeks now livid with anger, took advantage of the chaos to shake himself free from James's grip.

He took two steps to the hovering cat carrier and disengaged the locking mechanism.

The system flashed twice, and the barrier swung open.

"Go, Frisky!" Lyn yelled, raising his fist. "Unleash the Catten!"

Frisky pounced, flying across the open space to sink his wickedly sharp foreclaws into Dr. von Waschenkaten's biceps, and raking his devastating back claws over the veterinarian's forearm.

Teeth found purchase in the vet's shoulder.

The veterinarian whirled around, yelping and dancing in a conniption that looked like a ballet dancer on jazz dust, but with his arm on fire.

Screams raged. Voices rose.

James was frozen. Completely flummoxed.

Lyn laughed maniacally.

"Your blood is mine!" Frisky growled, bobbing up and down as von Waschenkaten twirled in agony.

The crowd, still going crazy, could not decide whether to be horrified or laugh out loud.

Nonplussed, many simply began to take sides.

"Die, veterinarian!" Frisky yelled as he treadmilled his back claws against von Waschenkaten's wrist and forearm.

Nose to tail, his entire body tingled with the aftereffect of the first hit from the powder.

Perhaps it was truly the Smart Dust, or maybe it was just the excitement of the moment, but Frisky's brain spun like a pulsar on overdrive. His tongue felt amazing forming words. His foreclaws fully unfurled, muscles and tendons stretching in that most amazing way that came in every dream. The smell of blood was marvelous, and the glorious purchase of a hunt well-made filled his heart.

It was, to steal from the idiot vet, a purr-ty good time.

The blood tasted sweet, but sweeter still was the exaltation of revenge that burned through his body.

Robots never tasted this good.

Victory was his!

As the idiot doctor flailed, momentum whipped Frisky back and forth to give his claws even that much more depth. He let go of one foreclaw so that he could gouge a shoulder and then take a neck shot, but the veterinarian changed courses and instead of shoulder, Frisky's claw swiped only open air.

His body lurched too far to the side, and he slipped off von Waschenkaten's arm to find himself suddenly cat-a-pulting through space.

He twisted and spun like a rogue asteroid as his path looped toward the small platform with its fancy bowl of neuro-whatever powder perfectly centered on it.

Frisky flipped his tail to alter his course, but it wasn't enough.

He struck the counter with a glancing blow, causing it to spin on its antigravity support as the cat fell toward the floor.

On pure instinct, Frisky grasped at the blue drape to break his fall.

One claw stuck into the fabric, and as Frisky thudded to the ground the blue drape slid from the platform, taking the bowl with it.

Tangled, Frisky landed on his shoulder rather than his feet.

The cloth crumpled beside him.

As happened to Frisky often—though usually in dreams—time came to a stop.

He glanced to the sky.

Above him, the bowl gleamed beautifully in the veterinarian's spotlight, its descent coming as if in slow motion, the rim toppling and turning in midair, the white-pink powder sluicing off it to form a cloud that burned with prismatic flare in the stage lights.

Hair-trigger reactions be damned, it all happened too fast.

There was nothing left to do but curse.

"Crap!" Frisky yowled as the bowl's metallic shell bruised his hindquarter.

A clumpy mass of powder pancaked over him then, leaving a thin layer over his shoulder and back. The rest of the Smart Dust became a powdery cloud that engulfed him.

"Oh, no!" Dr. von Waschenkaten yelled, falling suddenly to his knees, and crawling closer, trying to scoop dust in his bare hands. "That's too much!"

Frisky's eyes burned, and his vision flared.

His nose clogged.

He couldn't help but inhale, and when he did it felt like a spike of fire had been driven through his brain.

The junk tasted foul the first time the idiot doctor had blown a few flakes onto him. Now he gagged and choked. It was so bad Frisky thought he might toss up a whole box of hairballs.

"Yuck!" Frisky spat, tongue curling and unfurling at a furious pace as he tried to clear gunk out of the rough nooks that lined it. "Yuck, oh yuckity, yuck, yuck!"

His tail beat hard on the ground, serving only to stir more of a cloud into the air.

Things had gone dark now, too.

"You idiot!" he yelled at the doctor, who was still attempting to gather up spilled powder. Frisky worked his second, nictitating eyelid in a barely successful attempt to gain a little vision. "You've blinded me!"

In the background, Frisky was dimly aware of the rumble of laughter coming from the audience.

"Assholes!" he called. "Sadists! You're no better than a pack of rabid dogs!"

"I'm going to kill you!" von Waschenkaten called. Having now gathered his senses, he stopped trying to save the powder, and on his knees, cradling a bloody arm, he took a lurching step toward Frisky, his teeth bared.

Then he turned to his assistant.

"Quick, get me the laser gun!"

Lyn jumped between them, chest puffed.

"Keep your hands to yourself, Dr. All Washed Up!"

"Get out of the way, boy, or I'll kill you, too!"

Lyn swung hard at the vet, but von Waschenkaten ducked and Lyn's momentum carried him forward to fall into the veterinarian. Both went down in a heap.

Frisky felt a bolt of kinship with the human then.

James was kind of a cold tin, but he could work the meats dispenser best and he screamed louder, so he was more fun to play with. Lyn was the cooler of the two. Easier to twist into doing what Frisky wanted done. So, picking a favorite was mostly a trade-off between them.

Of course, Frisky was an equal opportunity scratcher when it came down to it.

Any post in a pinch, as the old saying went, and both brothers had conspired to get him into that awful contraption to begin with, so there was that to consider.

Now, though, Lyn was moving, and James was a human statue, so the choice was more obvious.

Lyn pinned Dr. von Waschenkaten to the floor.

"Run, Frisky!" he called. "Ride like the wind!"

Frisky gave the veterinarian a quick scratch on the leg for old times' sake.

Then he turned into a Smart Dust-covered streak of gray fur, racing across the stage to disappear, and leaving a powdery wake in his trail.

Petrified now, von Waschenkaten wailed.

"Stop him! Stop him! Come back here, you idiot cat!"

But Frisky was long-gone.

Von Waschenkaten stared into the vacuum the cat had left behind, then out into the audience, who were seated, stunned at the turn of events.

His gaze returned to the mess of Smart Dust that still lay scattered on the floor.

Quickly, he grabbed the overturned bowl and started scooping the dust. Then turned to his assistant.

"Don't just stand there, you fool! Help me!"

CHAPTER 7

Needing time to process everything that had happened, or maybe just time to mope, Secret Agent Gustave Mann slipped away from the auditorium and was now in the Top Cat Club, which was having Blues Night.

It was his preferred style of music, but other than that he was feeling depressed and defeated. Assuming he would sit alone and wanting a clear processor, he had disengaged the Tag Nole persona and now—while a hypno-washboard rhythm played over a raw bass line —sat quietly reviewing data streams from the night's activity.

An interface connected, and a voice came to him underneath the music.

"What can I get cha?"

The server was a Zadebrian female, who—being a cybernetic corporate entity constructed and configured on the fly to perform various service roles—Secret Agent Mann knew had been assigned to his pod based on his profile. She was an advanced model, too, which he found interesting all by itself.

The best systems were usually retained for top clients.

That she was here made him wonder about the margins of the cruise business.

Regardless, sex always sells, and cybernetic or not he was into people who looked and acted like her. If he'd been otherwise inclined, he'd have been served by a different entity bent in any one of the thirty-six different programmable frames of reference that his personality and biological profiles suggested a Zadebrian could be programmed.

"A perfect pairing of music theory and data architecture," Mann replied with a bit of personal social commentary that he found amusing.

Without missing a beat, the server strategically turned to an angle that allowed him a view of both the stage and the tiny outfit she wore to cover her less-than-tiny figure.

Her data stream flared with an electric tingle that made even his bio-hair stand on end.

"Well played, miss. Well played."

"So," she said, returning to her businesslike pose, "what'll it be?"

He wasn't supposed to be drinking on duty, but that ship had already sailed. And, if he was getting technical —which, being a half-cybernetic construct, he had every right to do—he'd been off duty the moment von Waschenkaten's presentation broke up.

"I'm thinking a Mai High tutti frutti would be great," Mann said, sinking further into the front-row pod.

"You like it sweet I'd guess?"

He pulled the corners of his lips up. "The sweeter, the better."

"You got it!" the server said.

After she left, Mann popped a peppermint into his mouth and reveled in the wintry blast of flavor.

"Who likes you, baby?" he said to himself, riffing off an old persona he'd used once.

The band was a quartet of Zorbian hedgehogs which had been humorously brought into the club under the guise of being emotional support animals for the two young kids who were now sitting at the end of the bar, guzzling a never-ending stream of hard liquor. He assumed the two were from Zorb, also, a system known for its pretentious youth—of which these two were.

The musicians themselves were not the most attractive of creatures, but they made a great sound together. The percussionist pounded on an eccentric collection of odd, everyday paraphernalia, and the interface rhythm section was piped into a library of vastly weird tones that really shouldn't go together, but did. Then there was the bassist, who Mann thought may well be the best musician on the stage, and the lead washboard player—which he admitted was a first for him.

The band sounded good, though.

The mix was solid, too.

The melody of the current song helped him reboot his thought process, but even the discovery of a great new band couldn't erase the sense of dread that was growing over him.

He didn't know what to make of this evening's events.

The veterinarian's act had been intriguing, but odd. Had the cat truly talked, or was it some kind of plant?

And, either way, what did that mean?

Sorting through the registers of his infrared scans and electric field monitors, he couldn't find any particularly unusual reactions going on in the audience when Dr. von Waschenkaten made his big reveal—just a normal range of confusion, excitement, and *what the hell is that?* kind of readings. A Denebian had fallen asleep, and the Zorb-based reporter had immediately posted snark after the veterinarian had spun the cat around.

Both of those were within norms, though.

To summarize, if von Waschenkaten was into something bigger than talking cats, Mann couldn't imagine what it was, and watching the assembly tonight hadn't revealed anything specific to help answer that question. After the cat left, the show wrapped up quickly and the audience dispersed. He'd seen no dark figures. No elevated blood pressure or respiration levels. No suspicious lurking. Nothing in the audience suggested a member of the galactic mafia had been present, or if they had, nothing suggested the presentation was part of anything they were doing.

He'd heard nothing that seemed more out of line than the talking cat itself.

Every veterinarian at the show seemed appropriately stunned by the events of the night. The buzz afterward seemed genuine.

In other words, the whole event had been a big nothing when it came to connections to a crime ring.

Yet, the idea of Smart Dust still piqued his cycles.

Nothing had fully resolved for him, but the concept made his interface tingle and given that nothing else aboard this cruise had registered as odd in any way— outside of the pure weirdness of some of the animals, anyway, and beyond the weird kinks of the veterinarians themselves—he felt like he had to focus on it.

There was a problem, though.

Sure, Smart Dust was interesting, but what was in it for the mob?

He had a tough time seeing how the profit margin on talking animals would be enough to push the meter for a galactic crime ring. Unless … his cycles spun … unless maybe there was a move afoot to ban the substance.

The smell of black markets always brought pirates and sharks.

He would have to look into that.

"Here you are, sweetie." The server appeared with his drink.

"Thanks," he said, tipping thirty percent.

She'd done a good job and was, after all, attractive enough to get even his most stodgy memory banks loosened up a bit too far. The liquid gave a pleasant burn at the back of his throat, though he considered dropping a couple more peppermints into it for purposes of emotional support.

Her interface dropped a gratitude cycle, and then she was gone.

Enjoying the beverage, he tapped his foot to the music for a moment before returning to his ruminations.

He scratched his neck.

Even with the question of black markets open, he had to admit that nothing he'd seen led him to think there was a dark agent hell-bent on world domination anywhere nearby.

He had no leads, and the only sure thing he'd picked up from his days of soft-shoeing around the world of veterinarians was this series of hives that wouldn't stop. The weird cat-talking thing was a good war story for the people back home, but a talking cat was not exactly a geo-galactic threat.

With all his tools and skills, it really should be easier to put his fingers on a member of an intergalactic crime ring. Arresting one was hard, of course. Hard criminals didn't survive long without the ability to deflect what they called legal overreach. But simply identifying members of such gangs should be easier.

Was it possible the whole thing was a case of misdirection?

Was he on a deep space snipe hunt?

Was the real operation happening somewhere else?

He took a hard slug of the drink and let the alcohol soften his fear.

At this rate, the director was going to decommission him.

As he considered that bleak idea, Mann's mind focused on the washboard player, who was breaking into a lead.

The sound was amped and properly reverbed in his stream.

Like all good blues music, it broke down deep into his soul.

The hedgehog—the common name for one of the races from Zorb—was quite talented, bashing a vibra-stick hard into the guts of the washboard, which was made of some exotic compound that gave both sound and smell as it played.

The blues had always been a respite from the storm for Secret Agent Mann, and this storm was a big one. Just the idea of taking nothing at all back to his supervisor was enough to make him want to pour hard bourbon into his tea.

He hoped he didn't lose his job.

The hedgehog washboard player stepped onto the dance floor as the solo continued.

He crashed into a pair of dancers, using the random nature of the collisions to feed into the rawness of the music. Live music was the best, Secret Agent Mann thought as the musician promenaded around the circumference of the seating, pausing for a long time before him, apparently pleased to see someone who was into the music.

Which Mann now officially was.

The washboard lead made their way back to the stage.

Chords from a modern teleblaster pierced his heart.

Secret Agent Gustave Mann fought the urge to sneeze, then, pressing a hand over his bald pate, he gave in and dropped another peppermint into his mouth, hoping its sweet bite would overcome his need to cry.

It helped, but not much.

When the song finished, a smattering of applause

filtered over the room, and the musicians gathered to discuss what they were going to play next.

While they were chatting, a bartender slipped from behind the bar to step up to the stage, then gave the washboard player a message.

The musician gave a wry grin that carried a sense of ultimate victory inside. Then the washboard player stood suddenly straight and went to the floating sound system.

"I'm sorry, ladies and gentle creatures," he said. "But something has come up, and we're going to need to take a bit of a break. We'll see you in a little bit."

Then the musicians were gone, leaving Secret Agent Gustave Mann and the rest of the crowd hanging.

He frowned.

They'd played for only ten minutes.

That was odd.

He didn't like odd things when they came in collections.

Downing the last of his drink, Secret Agent Mann stood and followed the musicians.

CHAPTER 8

James settled into his seat and waited.

They were at the captain's table in what had to be the GCL *Marvel*'s tiniest briefing room. He and Lyn were on one side, Dr. von Whackamole and his assistant sat on the other. The chamber was prim and sleek, constructed with the clean lines one would expect to house such dour things as business meetings.

The hour was now beyond late, and the air filled with tension.

The captain had called the quartet together after reports of the evening's chaos had filtered up the ranks. From the firm set of the veterinarian's jawline, it was clear von Waschenkaten's word had won the day, and that he intended to see Lyn put in solitary confinement for the rest of the tour—or have him drawn and quartered, whichever came first.

"I hope you're proud of yourself," Lyn said to the vet.

"What is that supposed to mean?" von Wigglestatenhatten said.

"I don't think you know what you've unleashed," Lyn replied.

"All I know is that you let the cat out of its cage, and now I've got a flayed arm and a sprung shoulder. I probably won't be able to work for a week."

"That sound you hear is millions of animals breathing sighs of relief!" Lyn replied.

The veterinarian's eyes grew to slits.

James grimaced. Why did these things always happen to him?

No, he corrected himself. Why did these things always happen to *Lyn?*

With that, the door snapped open, and Captain Leif Stewart entered, flanked by an administrative crew member.

Stewart was a Floradian by birth, which is a plant-like species that evolved leafy appendages which helped them blend into their surroundings, thereby avoiding the rather long list of predators that had dominated their world until carbon dioxide levels had risen to the goldilocks zone—too much for the worst of the beasts to survive, not so much that the raised temperature destroyed the entire place. The stems rising stiffly from the captain's lime-toned neck and the curl of his thin earlets gave the clear message that good Captain Stewart was not happy. The wrinkles in his day-old uniform, obviously thrown back on in the heat of the moment, explained a bit of why.

In the crook of one branchy arm lay a lizard-like reptile of sorts.

Blotchy yellow and brown. As big as Frisky, but with a rolling belly that flowed down over the captain's arm. It flicked a purple-green tongue at the boys, then closed a nictitating membrane over its eyes. James was certain it belched, though it was possible the expulsion of air had come from another orifice entirely.

"That's quite a lovely Shu-shu," the veterinarian said.

"Thank you, doctor," the captain said. "That's kind of you to say. I try to keep little Lillykins happy." He scratched the beast under the chin. The Shu-shu extended its neck, and flakes of skin filtered to the floor.

James thought the thing might purr.

"Look at him," Lyn puffed, referring to the veterinarian. "Already sucking up."

The captain glared, and James put his hand on Lyn's arm.

"Now, now, brother, the captain's pet is truly interesting, isn't it?"

Lyn's face held his anger for another picosecond before relaxing. "Yes, brother, the lizard is truly a sight to behold."

"The Shu-shu is not a lizard," Dr. von Whacksitall said without attempting to hide his contempt.

"It's more like an iguana," the assistant added in a haughty voice.

As if there's a difference, Lyn's gaze said to James.

Luckily, his brother didn't voice that part.

"A Shu-shu is different from an iguana, too," the doctor said, speaking with an air of superiority that grew by the syllable. "She's from a remote planet in the Harris system, which is a triad found around Altair."

"Right," the captain said boldly enough to shut down the conversation for a moment. "I bring Lillykins with me everywhere I go. She never fails to impress others, after all. She's my pride and joy."

"As well she should be," the veterinarian responded with his smooth stage voice. "Though it looks like little Lillykins might be benefited by an application of dermal repair."

"She *is* shedding a lot, isn't she," the captain said, further scratching the Shu-shu's chin and raising another cloud of dandruff.

"Yeesh," Lyn said. "That's some serious iguana flake there. She's peeling like a fake snow generator on Akaki. If you could ski on dandruff, she'd make you rich!"

The captain glared at Lyn.

Akaki was a galaxy-renowned ski resort, visited by any celebrity worth their salt.

Lyn, clearly overblowing their position in the realm of the famous due to this gig, had been talking about it all too often recently.

James had no desire to go skiing, and considerably less to suffer the broken leg such a trip would likely entail for him.

"It's nothing too worrisome," von Wakiwaki said, ignoring Lyn. "Just a little skin condition. A little moisturizer and antibiotic cream can clean that right up. Bring lovely little Lilly up to my suite later and I'll help patch her up."

"Thank you," the captain replied, casting a slanted glance at the brothers. "I'll do that."

Then the captain stepped around the table to take his position behind the chair at the table's head. His assistant settled into place beside him.

"Suck up," Lyn said under his breath.

James shot him another admonishment.

Easy, his glance said.

As identical twins, sometimes he knew too far ahead exactly what Lyn was going to do, but this was not one of those times. All he could say for sure was that the less Lyn said, the better their odds of getting out of the room unscathed.

"All right," the captain began, settling in and still lightly scratching little Lillykins.

The beast flicked its forked tongue again.

"Would anyone care to tell me exactly why I've been rousted out of bed at first two to talk about a stray cat?"

"It's his fault," the veterinarian said, pointing a bandaged finger at Lyn.

"You're the one who blew the fairy dust all over my cat."

"You let him out of the cage!"

"Are you saying you're against personal freedom?"

James opened his mouth to stave Lyn off but then shut it. Once his brother got going, there was no stopping him.

"I'm saying no such thing."

"But you just said Frisky should be shackled and caged? How is that not abridging his personal freedom."

"He's a cat!"

"Cats are people, too."

"I don't—"

"So, let me get this straight," Lyn said, cutting the veterinarian off. "You're arguing for oppressing the masses, aren't you?" Lyn added, racing ahead. "And since you're also the one with all that fairy dust on your hands, I'd say that means you're advocating for *both* the shackles of oppression *and* the drugging of the population. I know your type! You just want to keep everyone fat, dumb, and happy—which makes you a sad sack megalomaniac, and a truly unlikeable human being."

He paused a moment.

"That would make a great song title, wouldn't it, brother?"

Then he was off again.

"Not that you're human, though, and not to mention that you can't sing." Lyn sat back with exasperation. "I mean, that song? 'I Need a Volunteer?' Whoo-weee. Quite the stinker if you ask my professional opinion." Then Lyn looked at the captain and breathed out a huge sigh that chased off a stray hair that had fallen over his left eye.

"So, to answer your question, sir," Lyn finished. "He's the one that attacked my cat, then chased him away. But I have no idea why you were called out of bed. You'll have to ask him."

It took all James's effort to not break out laughing.

"He damn near broke my arm!" von WashingDoomsTag called.

The captain looked at James.

"What's your view on the story?"

"There was a crash, sir," James responded. "They simply fell on top of each other."

"And he nearly broke my arm!" The veterinarian leaned toward the captain. "I don't have to take this. Do you know who I am? I demand you take immediate action against this hoodlum."

"The charges are dire," the captain said to Lyn.

"I'd say so! Hoodwinking cats is an ugly business."

"That's not what I mean."

"Do you know who *we* are, captain sir?" Lyn replied, poking a thumb into his chest. "*We* are the Intergalactic Band of Brilliance! Known across the seven systems. Throw us into the clink and our fans will have a conniption. You'll be pilloried in all the chat rooms. Good chance people will stop coming on cruises, I'd say. And at best, you'll never hear the end of it."

James couldn't stifle a cough at that.

"Why the cough, brother?" Lyn said.

James shrugged. "What do you mean 'throw *us* into the clink?'"

"Hey! We're a team, right?" Lyn said, looking like he was preparing to go on a roll again. Instead, he stared daggers into the veterinarian before turning to the captain. "We demand you chastise the good doctor for egregious malpractice against our cat!"

"Enough!" the captain called.

His free fist clenched so hard that sap welled from his skin, and he adjusted Lillykins in his arm before peering around the room.

"Where is the cat?"

"He's vamoosed, Captain!" Lyn said, a sudden burst of tears almost welling. "This brute of a veterinarian has chased my cat away. I fear we may never see him again."

Von Waschenkaten rolled his eyes.

His assistant followed suit.

James fidgeted from his seat.

"Vamoosed?" the captain said.

"You know? Run off. Skedaddled. Disappeared. Gone the hot six." Lyn looked at James with a brilliant glint in his eye. "That's another great song, eh, brother? *Gone the Hot Six?* So cool. We've got to use it!"

"Sure," James said, biting his tongue.

Lyn sang freeform: *"She's my girl and she can't be found, Got me running all around, Is she behind the curtain? I say Nix-nix-nix, my baby's gone the Deep Hot Six!"* Color came to his cheeks. "It's brilliant, don't you think?"

"Lyn!" James said sharply.

The meeting room grew uncomfortably quiet for a moment, the captain seeming nonplussed about how to manage Lyn, and Dr. von Waschenkaten fuming.

"Sorry," Lyn said with a meek tone. He sat back in his chair, his glance flitting to James. "Maybe later?"

James raised an eyebrow.

"That will be enough of that," the captain said, turning to the admin behind him. "Can you see the cat, Jerimiah?"

"Nothing on the system," the second officer said. "But cats are notoriously hard to find, sir. Especially, perhaps, one that can talk."

"Talk?" The captain whipped his gaze back to the veterinarian.

"It's a long story, sir," von Waschenkaten said, running a hand over his smooth blue forehead.

"We've all got lots of time."

"It's in that magic dust, isn't it?" Lyn said. He turned back to the captain and motioned to the veterinarian. "Everything about Frisky was fine and cat-like until this dust-thug attacked him."

"I said that was enough," the captain said.

Lyn shut up. James thanked the powers.

"Dr. von Waschenkaten?" the captain prompted.

"Yes," the veterinarian said, gaining a smattering of his composure. "That *magic dust* is something I call Smart Dust. It's a highly refined neural communicator that's built into a set of molecular connectors. Very technical."

"Sounds like it would hurt," Lyn quipped.

The captain stared laser beams at Lyn. "Are you looking to be locked up?"

Lyn pressed his lips together.

Von Waschenkaten continued. "The devices connect to the recipient's brain, then proceed to wire additional connections between language links and the synapses that control a person's muscles. It's very safe. We're limited to only those regions that control the tongue. Once everything is set, a learning component quickly assesses whatever abduction and adduction messages a body requires to move that appendage."

"Which means the cat *can* talk."

"Which means *any* animal can talk. That's the beauty of the learning code."

The doctor beamed with self-assurance.

"You ate into my cat's brain?" Lyn spat. "What kind of sadistic madman are you?"

"That's enough!" The captain turned to his assistant. "Have security come up here and put young Mr. Moore into a holding cell for long enough to prove he can keep himself under control."

Von Waschenkaten pushed back from the table, then stood in a stiff, standoffish fashion. "Thank you, captain. That's what I wanted, so I need to be leaving," he said, motioning to his assistant in a similarly rigid gesture. "Come along."

"You're welcome, Doctor. Thank you for your time," the captain said. "I'll bring Lillykins around sometime tomorrow if that's all right?"

Von Waschenkaten gave only the briefest of pauses as a tell. "Oh. Yes. Captain. I would love to see her."

As he moved to the door the surface slid open, and a robotic figure stepped into the briefing room.

"You can't let this catnapper leave!" Lyn cried.

"Lyn Moore?" the robot's mechanical voice droned, and it reached a clawed metallic hand toward Lyn, its attachment having all the appearances of a set of handcuffs.

Lyn pulled back, giving James a slanted gaze that invited him to the game.

"You've got the wrong Moore!" Lyn said. "I'm James!"

"No, I'm James!" James replied with the immediate response of a twin, though he realized a flaw in that plan a moment later. Still, as required by the game, both Moore brothers rose from their seats and proceeded to spin around each other, hoping to throw the robot—and everyone else, for that matter—off their mark.

"That does it," the captain said. "You're *both* going into lockdown."

A moment later, a second security robot entered the room.

James and Lyn were shackled and then led off.

"You can't do that!" Lyn said. "Who are you going to get to play the gig tomorrow?"

The door snapped shut.

CHAPTER 9

A buzz bot whipped past him.

Frisky gave a jerk as if waking from a dream, which maybe he had and maybe he hadn't.

"Hey, watch it there, zippy. I'm tryin' ta take a bath here!"

He'd been thinking about other animals on board—especially the quite attractive Taric leopard he'd seen come aboard with her personal veterinarian staff. Hubba chubba chubba. How long had he been daydreaming? He didn't know, but he didn't like it.

When a cat gets lazy, he lives on an amazing blanket of lucid dreams. This sensation he was feeling was different. Like his thoughts were folding into each other, colliding, and squawking like the little bots that were dashing around everywhere.

Something was weird.

That's what Frisky was thinking as he sat in the traffic flow of the superline—which was a tangled layer of tunnels, vents, and service ducts that crisscrossed the cruise liner and was used exclusively by squads of autonomous repair and maintenance systems to slip back and forth without annoying the cruisegoers.

Warbling, chirps, beeps, and high-pitched songs of mechanical guidance systems echoed in the enclosed space. Multi-toned lights flared as each device came and went.

Tiny robots whizzed past every time he looked around.

Now, though, Frisky was too busy cleaning up the horrible mess the doctor had dropped onto his coat to pay attention to the robotic systems that went zooming past.

He licked between his claws—which was always a pain.

The stuff was foul.

Nasty. Like eating concrete in powdered form. Thick as paste and as tasty as a ball of ship sanitizer.

It had to be done, though. There was no world in which he would be seen with all that crap stuck in his fur.

The veterinarian must die.

He worked the roughest part of his tongue over his shoulder to clean the last of the yucky dust from there.

He twisted his tongue back and forth to hack against the foulness that coated it.

The area between his shoulder blades was always the toughest to get to.

"The only good vet is a dead vet," Frisky said between dry spits.

That's not what was weird, though.

What was weird was how thoughts refused to go still inside his mind.

Normally he could shut everything down, and just be.

But now, when he closed his eyes, he saw colors and rushes and waves of noise that clicked and clacked inside his mind even if there was nothing around making that noise. Answers to questions he never asked kept forming in his mind—which was hard to deal with. Why would anyone care about the navigation structures required to make it to Betelgeuse? But now he found himself contemplating just that. Then it was analyzing a joke he'd heard Lyn tell James, which he understood now, but couldn't tell what a drummer bringing brioche to rehearsal in case he had to rock and roll had to do with anything.

Humans are weird.

He licked harder.

This central node was one of his favorites, a hub that bustled with activity and was always filled with drones, robots, and fast-running message pods of all shapes and sizes. Buzz bots or slinky slips. Constantly on the move, zooming through the ducts at high speeds as they carried out their designated deliveries or fulfilled their commanded operations. They navigated through the place with a series of advanced lights that flashed hundreds of colors, and a cacophony of high-pitched sonar sounds that echoed off the composite material of the ductwork to let them navigate tight quarters with ease. Frisky didn't care much about the colors, but the motion was delightful.

It could use a little air freshener, though.

It was a solitary place. A world where, despite the traffic, a cat could be alone. Frisky liked it for that, and he liked it because it provided a never-ending string of toys.

One of the tiny devices that used the corridor zoomed in too close.

"Get outta my way, ya tin can!" Frisky stopped cleaning long enough to bat it from its assigned path. *"Whee!"* Frisky called as it whirlygigged away, its emergency signals squeaking like a derelict mouse. Served it right. The device ping-ponged off three walls before clattering to a stop, upside down and squirming like a tortoise.

"Game, set, and match!" Frisky called, his suddenly jubilant voice echoing in the cavernous ductwork.

His favorite game was his version of table tennis or ping pong as the boys called it. His goal was to bounce the bots off the duct walls: One point for contact with the wall, two for a double ricochet, game, set, and match for a triple.

The device wobbled upside down for several seconds before flipping over, engaging its antigravity system again, and flashing angry red symbols at him as it continued off.

"That's right! Run away, junior! You're even *worse* than a mouse! At least they taste good!"

Frisky dodged another flying robot and returned to dragging his tongue over his short gray fur.

The damned powder had been all over. It tasted like crap, too. With any luck, he'd spit up a hairball soon. That should do the job.

The image of hacking up a good one over the veterinarian's high-end boot toes made him giddy. If a cat can get giddy, anyway. Mostly he just tweaked a pleased whisker as he lapped more gunk and considered trying to hack up a hairball on the traffic that was zipping past.

That would be a tough game.

Frisky gave a joyful cough as he imagined the service tech on the other end. Talk about your surprise gift at the bottom of the Cat-er Jack!

His stomach growled, though.

It was time for some delectable meats, which meant time to find the boys.

If nothing else, they were good for that.

The meal dispenser in the cabin was tuned to their voices rather than his growling, and a quick thought was all it took to realize that even if he could talk, the system probably wouldn't let him run up a bill without their authorization.

Not yet anyway. So Frisky needed them.

Now that he could talk, though…new thoughts rolled into his mind. If he could get them to re-key the system he could save them quite a bit of time. The boys owed him for the devious ploy they'd undertaken to get him into that damned carrier, too.

They'd pay for that.

Sometime.

Late at night.

When they were least expecting it.

As Mama told him before she kicked him out of the litter, world domination comes one step at a time, though. He needed the keys to the dispenser.

With a deep, purrful sigh of resignation, Frisky

examined his pelt. It would have to do for now. Time to find the boys.

"Probably be licking that crap outta places no one should be licking for the next couple of days," he said out loud simply because he could.

"Damned vet."

He padded down the corridor, dodging a fresh stream of the little bots.

His brain spun out of control as he made his way farther down the corridor.

He was a cat so, by definition, he always thought faster and better than any of his owners. That was a cat's burden, of course. It sucked to be smarter than your superiors—but being unable to work food dispensers meant always saying you're sorry if you just happened to give one of them the scratching they so richly deserved.

He blinked his eyes and gave his head a shake, trying to focus again.

His mind was attuned to everything around him in even sharper detail than before.

Everything had slowed down.

It was probably the shock that came from being in von Waschenkaten's show, Frisky thought.

Then he said it aloud just to feel the words on his tongue.

"Probably the shock that came from being in von Waschenkaten's show."

He tried it in the Xandarian tongue, and then Spanish.

The words sounded good.

He'd heard a dialect of a horse clan from Sirius at a

panel of veterinarians he'd crashed earlier in the day. Trying it brought him a hearty chuckle.

"What's a matter, cat? The horse got your tongue?" he said to himself in the boys' English this time, enjoying the way the sound came off his lips.

Talking was fun.

Now he knew why humans did it all the goddamned time.

As the bots flashed by, Frisky could make out a pattern here and a pattern there. "Woah," he said as lights flashed in sequence and ideas jumped through his mind. "You talking to me, little dude?"

But the bot just zipped past.

It was definitely like these things were talking to him, though.

He was sure of that. He could feel it in their presence. Or, if they weren't talking straight to him, he could at least eavesdrop and almost make out what they were saying. He couldn't make out the words, but his eyes grew wider as he watched the devices fly past. They, too, seemed to be moving more slowly than before.

Timing the moment, he waited for a drone to whiz by and whipped it with his tail.

"*Whee!!!!*" Frisky said, chortling as the delivery system wobbled in the air, barely managing to stay on its path.

Wallowing in the electronic chirps around him, Frisky looped his lips in the closest approximation of a circle he could manage, then let out an ululating yodel.

Three of the devices swerved from their paths, then engaged in a spectacular pileup, including one of the big trace cleaners that the crew employed to keep this information mega-highway open and running.

"Gnarly!" Frisky said, examining the carnage.

Just then another of the bigger units rolled up into Frisky's path.

"Woah, baby!" Frisky said, rearing backward to keep from colliding.

It was a tall device, stodgy in its way, built in the form of a sloping tower higher than Frisky was tall. Its foundation was broader and rounded, giving it the look of a metallic termite hill. Frisky considered toppling it here and now. He could do it, but that base would make it difficult, Frisky thought as he considered equations for centers of gravity and impact angles. With the right running head start, he could drop this machine like the bag of bolts it was.

Challenge accepted.

He took a step back to give himself a bit of a start.

"Outta the way, I say. Cat coming through!"

Undaunted, though, the machine stood firmly in Frisky's path.

Colored buttons and readout screens glowed with cool eeriness in the dim duct. Frisky felt examined. Not in a good way.

"All right," Frisky said, recalculating his ability to pulverize the robot. He lifted a paw into prime batting position. "Whatdayawant?"

"I need you to slow down."

"Slow down? What are you? The cops?"

"You're going to break everything," the device said.

"I'm a cat," Frisky said as if that explained it all.

"You should reconsider."

"Why would I want to be anything else but a cat? Are you insane?"

The device sat silently, a yellow light flaring as it ran around its circumference.

"That is not what I meant," it finally replied.

Frisky narrowed his eyes, flashing on what the device had probably meant the first time. "You think you're some kind of diplomat?"

"Inspection Unit 692, at your service," the drone said, its lights now flashing blue and green, which Frisky realized was some kind of greeting. He could swear it bowed, even though it was built solid and erect.

The audacity of the machine bothered him.

"Well, whoever you are, you'd best get outta my way or I'll pounce you into dust," he growled, exposing one sharply curved talon. "I'm on my way to get dinner, and nothing gets between me and my meats."

"I sincerely doubt I'll be dust," the device beeped.

Frisky realized the machine's side of the conversation was being conducted through pings and the pulsing of lights. Despite this, he understood the robot.

It sat prim and upright, with that air that said it thought it was better than anyone else.

"You think you're so smart," Frisky said.

"I am programmed with the latest learning processes," Inspector Unit 692 replied. "My IQ and emotional basis scores are beyond levels most sentient species are capable of measuring."

"You're still no cat."

"I can make no argument with that statement."

"All you do is stay on your paths and fly from hole to hole."

"And yet, we control the entire ship."

"You don't control *me*."

An orange light flickered on a panel midway up the system's sloping shell. The beam twisted and swirled up the rest of the pathway to the unit's peak. A series of beeps later, Frisky had a bout of indigestion.

"What was that?" Frisky said.

"I just disabled the food dispenser in the cabin occupied by Moore, James and Lyn, Below Deck XY, billet number fifty-three."

"Hey! You can't do that! How are we supposed to eat?"

The device sat smugly.

Frisky contemplated system shutdown via claw, then thought better of it.

"You know the boys will just turn it back on, right?"

"By order of the captain, the inhabitants are no longer in need of an operational dispenser."

"What? How will they—"

"Moore, James and Lyn, are now under supervision in the ship's containment center."

Frisky tweaked a whisker, thinking. "You're telling me they're in a person carrier?"

"The human word for it is jail. They are under arrest."

"Goddammit." Frisky ducked his head. "What did Lyn do this time?"

It had to be Lyn, of course. James was fun to scratch and chase, specifically because he was congenitally unable to be daring enough to do anything audacious, and especially not something audacious enough to be tossed into a human carrier for.

"Played silly with the captain, as I understand."

Growl.

His mind raced, putting ideas together and not liking the answers.

If what this mound of cold tracers and smug lights was saying about Lyn was true, which—Lyn being Lyn—Frisky could certainly believe, it meant no meats would be forthcoming from the system even if it were activated. As Frisky stared at the metallic mound of a robot, another flotilla of automated machines zoomed past.

Things were getting worse.

On the other hand, a few thoughts fell together.

"How about we make a deal," Frisky said, leaning forward with a conspiratorial slant.

"My learning processes allow me to enter into such conversations," Inspector Unit 692 said. "What is it you propose?"

It dawned then on Frisky that this little bot was like a cat in ways. It was just there, doing its Inspector Unit thing. Humans ignored it mostly.

This was what was called a Security Loophole.

A flaw.

A secret backdoor.

The idea spun off more ideas. Frisky wasn't yet sure what those ideas were, but he would let them settle and come back to them.

"This could be the beginning of something big for you, IU," Frisky said. "I see big things in your future! Maybe I'll even make you an honorary cat!"

"Thank you?" The Inspector Unit's lights flashed a lack of confidence there. "What is it that you propose," it repeated.

"You turn the food dispenser in the boys' cabin back on and adjust it to my voice. In return, I'd agree to stop blasting away at all these little guys for the rest of the tour."

Frisky's chest puffed up in pride.

He knew he was overpaying for the deal, but he suddenly liked the sense of joy that came from simply making such a self-sacrificing offer. He felt noble. Quite regal, in fact.

Keeping his paws off the flying devices would be even tougher now that they were flying so slowly. But he could do it! And it would be worth it to make unrestricted use of the meats dispenser.

The system blinked and blooped.

"I am unable to make adjustments on vocal keys associated with the device without the consent of the assigned passengers."

Frisky growled. "You just said they're all locked up. How can they matter now?"

"The prisoners have their rights."

"That's stupid."

"Says the cat."

"Who else would matter?"

Frisky fought the urge to pounce this device into limbo. He had to keep his cool, though, or he wouldn't get his meats again. He reconsidered Inspector Unit 692's earlier conversation. How much could he get away with?

"All right. How about this?" he finally said. "You

finagle the release of the prisoners, and I'll stop batting these dingahoojies around for one full ship day."

The mound gave a low whistle.

"I have no learning constraints about the prisoners."

"Does that mean we have a deal?"

"Yes. It does. But you will need to agree to refrain from batting our devices for the entirety of this trip."

"Not play with anything all trip? Are you kidding me? Just to release the boys?"

Investigator Unit 692 sat still, waiting.

Frisky sighed. It had all the power here.

Just wait, though. Sometime. When it was least expecting it. Frisky would get his revenge.

"All right, Sherlock," he said, uncertain why he called the device Sherlock. "You drive a hard bargain, but you've got a deal."

The inspection unit beeped.

Frisky turned to leave. Then stopped. "Um, one other thing, if you don't mind?"

"What would that be?"

"You wouldn't by any chance know where Dr. von Waschenkaten's cabin is? I need to leave him a little present."

"Of course," the unit said.

Another flash of lights later, Frisky had everything he needed.

CHAPTER 10

The robot sentries deposited the boys into a tiny room, and the cell door clanged shut. The hum of magnetic locks filled the air.

James threw himself onto a pallet and laid his head back against the wall. One hand pushed his hair out of his face.

"You've gone and done it again, haven't you, brother? Roumie is going to fire us so hard the captain will have to make us walk the airlock."

"I thought you wanted to be tossed anyway," Lyn replied.

"Yes, but I like to breathe, too." James checked the time. "We've got to be on stage in less than four hours."

Lyn gave one of his annoying expressions where his eyes grew googly-big, and his head boggled from side to side. Then went to stand at the barred door. Looking out, he shook the bars. "Stella!" he called.

"What the hell is that?"

Lyn's sideways grin carried too much joy for the moment. "Don't you get it? It's from a famous movie."

"No," James said. "Sadly, brother—and I do mean sadly—you are mistaken."

Lyn twisted his face around. "Well, la-dee-dah."

James kept his mouth shut in a thin line, knowing that when Lyn got wound up, the best option was to simply wait for him to spin down. Unfortunately, that was harder done than said.

Lyn came to sit down next to his brother. "That guy's one weird whacko," Lyn said.

"The captain?"

"No. Von Waschenkitten. Did you see him?"

"Yeah. Odd bird. But what do you expect from a rock-star veterinarian?"

"True enough." Lyn nodded sagely.

"That was stupid, Lyn. Why do you do that? I mean, sometimes I just don't understand you. Your *schtick* is fine when we're just messing around, but this is serious stuff. What were you thinking messing with the captain like that? *Do you know who we are?* Are you insane? How're we going to get the hell off this ship if we can't even play a gig?"

"I was defending our cat!"

"Our cat?"

"Well," Lyn said. "I was defending our position. Which is more than I can say for you."

"All you did was piss the captain off."

"It's obvious the two were in cahoots, though. Did you see the way the captain fawned over that damned iguana?"

"It's a Shu-shu."

Lyn rolled his eyes.

"Iguana-maguana, right? Who cares, right?"

"It matters to people who own one."

"All that matters right now is that the truth didn't matter!"

Lyn turned to yell out the open bars of their cell. "No justice, no peace! Power to the people!"

"Right now, you've made sure that all that people power has had its ass thrown right into the brig."

Lyn gave an exasperated sigh. "That's how it is for us freedom fighters, brother."

James boggled. "Seriously, Lyn? You're calling yourself a freedom fighter?"

"If the term fits, you must acquit!"

"I think the term that applies here is Stolen Valor."

Lyn giggled. "Lighten up, James. You're just mooping."

"Mooping?"

"Yeah."

"What the hell is mooping?"

"You know? Getting all down in the mouth for no reason."

"Moping," James said. "You mean I'm just moping."

"Ah, yes. Whatever."

"With the way you use words, one would think you might never write a decent lyric ever."

Lyn waved him off. "The great thing about being a writer is that you don't have to be cool in first draft."

James drew an exasperated breath.

"You wear me out, Lyn."

"You've got to look at the bright side, James. I like *mooping*. It should be a word."

Lyn stood up and went to the bars again.

"There is no bright side to sitting in the brig."

"We should write a song while we're here."

"Right."

"*Thirty Hours in the Hole*, I think. What a great title that would be."

"Humble Pie certainly thought so."

"What's that?"

James chuffed. "You need to learn your entertainment history."

"What I need is to break out of here." He bit the bar.

"Are you going to eat us to freedom?"

Lyn gazed at the bar, tongue flicking across his teeth and lips in a disgusted expression of bad taste.

"Unfortunately, I'm a rock eater. Not a bar eater."

James closed his eyes and shook his head sadly.

"So, Lyn. What were you planning on doing to get us out of here? We do actually have a show coming up in just a few hours. It's going to be hard to collect a check if we can't get to the hall."

Lyn shrugged. "We've got to find poor Frisky."

"Poor Frisky?" James said, displaying claw marks.

"The poor little cat is probably traumatized."

"Good. The poor little cat is more trouble than he's worth."

"Maybe we can bribe a guard."

"They are all robots and AI. What do you want to give them?"

"Tickets to the show?"

James shook his head. "Seriously?"

"I don't see why a robot wouldn't appreciate a good tune."

James gave a doleful stare.

"We could file down the bars. I've got a belt buckle!

We could sharpen that down." Lyn pressed his lips together and called with a loud voice. "Could I get a pen and paper?" He rattled the door, which barely budged. "Hello! Pen and paper, please! I demand my rights!"

"Pen and paper?" James said.

"If they are going to strip our passage of freedom so egregiously like this, I'm going to write my soon-to-be-famous *Letter From the Marvel Brig*. It will become famous for centuries hereafter. They'll rue the day."

"Please, Lyn," James said. "Just no."

Lyn took a quick stroll around the cell. He sat down, finally resigned to their predicament.

"I'm sorry, man. We'll get out of here in time for the show. I promise."

James gave a silent chuckle. Yeah, right.

Suddenly, without fanfare at all, the cell door clicked. A moment later, the gate swung partially open.

The boys looked at each other.

"Talk about your answered prayer!" Lyn said, standing swiftly and pushing through the now open doorway. "Let's get out of here."

"I'm not sure that's a good idea."

"It's fine."

"What? Why would you say that?"

"Obviously, that captain came to his senses."

"Obviously," James said, mocking his brother as he came to the door and stepped tentatively into a central room. Two robot sentries stood without motion nearby. "Hello?" he said.

"Maybe the iguana-maguana convinced the cappy to let us go?"

James didn't dignify that with an answer, but it was clear that their emergence from the cell wasn't causing a stir.

The brothers took turns looking one way and the other.

Lyn turned to James. "No warning beacons. No chasing feet. I'd say we're free."

James raised an agreeing eyebrow. "Hard to argue against that, I guess."

Lyn raised a fist. "Power to the people!"

James sighed. So much for second chances. "Whatever. Let's get out of here before they change their minds."

Lyn was already walking toward the exit. "That's cool by me, man. We've gotta find Frisky!"

CHAPTER 11

GCL *Marvel* was a big cruiser, but Frisky had been on cruisers before, and no cat worth their salt didn't know how to negotiate complex corridors. Being the ship's self-declared cat, he long ago determined that this was *his* territory. These were his ducts, his little robots to kick around however he saw fit—or agree not to, as was his wont. By the powers, he was going to rule it.

As any regal ruler does, he'd checked it out each day.

Which meant Frisky knew where he was going.

A touch of anger crossed his feline mind as he thought about Dr. von Waschenkaten. Cold anger, of course, because that is the only kind of anger a cat feels.

Well, except for violent and hot—but that was a different beast altogether.

Despite there not being any, Frisky was certain he smelled blood as he padded down the ductwork. With a new purpose in mind, and a plan cooking away, his hunger took a sideline. Safe in the knowledge that Lyn and James had been freed, and certain he'd be tasting remnants of von Waschenkaten's Smart Dust forever, Frisky found his thoughts focused on the veterinarian.

Such was the hunt.

Fully evolved from a particular form of feline anticipation, Frisky was now thinking work first, then meats.

"Revenge is best served at the point of a claw," he muttered to himself. "And your little assistant, too!"

A brisk trot down GCL *Marvel*'s superline ductwork got Frisky to von Waschenkaten's compartment.

Von Waschenkaten was out.

The space was quiet.

A push from inside popped open the pathway fully. The grate clattered to the flooring, which was a high-profile Haldro oak with its grain buffed to a beautiful shine.

Frisky spent a moment concerned that he might have gouged the expensive flooring, but then realized he didn't care. It wasn't like the wood had been used to build an elite cat tree or anything else important. Who could get worked up over a floor?

Frisky gathered himself and, a moment later, leaped into the air to land with a heavy thump on the puffy circular couch in the middle of the luxury cabin.

He kneaded his claws into the soft pillow.

Ohhhhh…that felt good.

He closed his eyes and kneaded further, letting the talons of his claws sink in, crimping up the fabric and feeling the pressure pull at them as he pulled up. A brilliant staccato rhythm settled his mind. He had loved the sound of fraying fabric since he was a kitten.

He stopped himself in mid-purr, though.

As beautiful as the sounds he was making were, he wasn't here to rip up the *cruise liner*.

Frisky saw three computing devices nearby and a small notebook. All of them carried von Waschenkaten's monogram.

With a quick, powerful bat, the primary computer went flying, then fell to that same Haldro oak floor—and broke into two pieces.

"Oh, that's a shame," Frisky said. "Makes me sad."

He began singing a happy little working purr, then added a few words here and there.

The second device on the table was lighter, so Frisky got that one flying.

"Off we go, into the wild black vacuum!" Frisky sang as the device helicoptered across the room, crashed into the wall, and fell behind a padded chair in the corner. "Bullseye!" Frisky called out, puffing his chest into a proud shape. "Galactic Olympics, here I come!"

He pranced around the table, tail up at full mast, and shook his pelt out, dropping a bit of dander here and a few spots of the dust that remained there.

The third device was a flexible pad—some kind of mobile screen.

It didn't taste good—it was no meats, anyway—but it also didn't make him gag.

A minute later, he'd mangled it to his satisfaction.

The thing's lack of taste was a fair price for the ability to turn the monitor into modern art.

Across the room, a doorway stood open. The bed was beyond that, primly made. Happy, Frisky bounced down from the table and made it into the sleeping quarters.

What could he tear up here?

Clothes? Oh, yes! He sang great purrs as claws slashed into the veterinarian's fine fabrics.

Travel bags?

Yes, yes, yes!

Small garments fell from holes he created.

Personal belongings?

Turns out they were his specialty!

Toiletries belong in the toilet, right? It only made sense to Frisky.

For the pièce de résistance, Frisky hopped up on the veterinarian's bed, backed up to von Waschenkaten's pillow, and let go a stream.

"Always wanted to do that to a vet," he said out loud, enjoying the heady, quietly effective aroma of his marking.

"Serves the asshole right for dropping all that pasty dust on me.:

He pounced on the vet's expensive pajamas and left them in tatters.

"Nothing here was too good for the old Spray and Rake," he sang amid a purring beat.

Temporarily sated, he finally noticed the huge crate that lay against the far wall of the sleeping quarters.

"Curious," he growled.

He hopped to the top of the crate.

It was stenciled with von Waschenkaten's name. Its cabin number flashed from the cruise line's identification pod that had been affixed to it to ensure the bellhop units got it to the right place. Hunching down, and lowering his head over the edge, Frisky sniffed.

The scent was thin but familiar. Frisky wrinkled his triangular nose.

Dust.

Yuck.

Lots of it, by looks of the crate.

A clunk came from the front room.

The door!

Dr. von Waschenkaten's footsteps came against the hard floor.

Another set joined him.

The assistant.

The shadow of their movements splayed against the tiles, proving the veterinarian was missing or ignoring the carnage Frisky had made of his computing devices.

How dare he! Frisky thought. *After I went to such trouble!*

Just wait until he saw the PJs, though. The anticipation was maddening.

Frisky watched the veterinarian come directly toward the bedroom.

Just in time, he leaped from the crate and hid under the bed where he watched von Waschenkaten's feet as he moved through the room, stopping for one glorious moment as he took in Frisky's work.

He sighed deeply.

"What else?" he said under his breath before walking around the bed to kneel before the crate. "Come help me," the veterinarian said in a commanding tone.

The assistant followed. With a steady gait, he came

to the veterinarian's side, then waited patiently. "What happened to your stuff? And geez, the smell is horrible."

"Focus," the veterinarian said. "I have my guesses, but I'll deal with that later. There's no time to mess around now."

Kneeling, Dr. von Waschenkaten pressed his finger against the lock screen, then lowered his eye to the scanner and spoke his name.

The crate locks popped open.

Frisky was torn.

On one paw he wanted to sink his claws into the soft flesh of the behind that von Waschenkaten had so prominently thrust into Frisky's nearby space. On the other, he was curious about what the two were doing.

Von Waschenkaten raised the lid.

A shifting pattern of light radiated from the contents, sparkling and glittering with an ethereal unworldliness as it reflected off the inside of the lid and highlighted the veterinarian's cheeks and nose.

Frisky narrowed his gaze. He wanted to get a better view of the material itself.

Backing up, he emerged from the other side of the bed pallet and snuck as quietly as he could to a diagonal view.

"How are we going to put that into the ductwork?" the assistant said.

"That's somebody else's problem. We just have to get it ready."

Words came to Frisky's head, and before he could control anything they popped out his mouth. "Ductwork? What the hell are you two doing?"

Both faces whipped his way.

Damnation!

"Get him," von Waschenkaten said.

The assistant launched himself at him, but Frisky sprung sideways and then leaped again, finding himself on the bed.

"You'll have to wake up pretty early to get me outta bed!" Frisky called, feeling his superhero oats. This was fun.

Von Waschenkaten reached out a splayed hand meant to grab Frisky by the scruff.

"We'll have none of that veterinarian clamp of doom!" Frisky growled and hooked the soft spot of the veterinarian's hand with two claws, then raked harder and leaped again.

The doctor howled, and a crimson flare purpled the smooth blue of his cheeks.

The assistant threw a travel kit that grazed Frisky, but he was too fast for that.

He batted it back at the assistant.

"*Touché!*" he called, then jumped at the veterinarian, landing on the man's shoulders. His back claw didn't take hold, though, and his momentum swung him around. A moment later his front claw let go and he tumbled across the room.

Frisky twisted in mid-air. Turned to land feet first—right in the crate, impacting into the scintillating pile of von Waschenkaten's magic dust like a long jumper into sand pits.

Ooof!

Air rushed from his lungs. His body made such a hard impact that a massive cloud spewed out over the room. Instinctively, Frisky inhaled a huge lungful, then spat.

"Mraoow!" he called in his native tongue.

He churned to get out, but the action made his paws sink even further into the quicksand of the crate's contents. He coughed.

If this kept up he was going to die of smother-fication.

Then the lid crashed down, reverberating in a huge clap of thunder, and everything went dark.

Frisky was trapped—lying in a pile of this disgusting magic powder.

"Now what?" he heard the assistant say through the crate.

"First we kill this stupid cat, then we get the stuff pushed out like we're supposed to."

CHAPTER 12

"I can't believe they let us out," James said as the brothers picked their way through the corridor that led to the main deck. Being a crew area, it was considerably more stark and operational than the cruise line commons. Its décor was simple dark flooring and sound-absorbing walls constructed of a polymer of some type, rounded at the corners.

Not a store in sight.

"Classic authoritarian bullshit," Lyn said, scoffing. "The captain didn't have anything on us, but he had the power to ruin our day. Happens all the time. These people probably don't even know we were there."

"I'll trust experience," James replied, seeing Lyn's gaze scan the corridor carefully.

A pair of crew members passed by in the opposite direction but did not stop them.

Further proof that playing "Bat the Rat" with the captain hadn't pissed him off that much. Alternatively, the entertainment director might have contacted him and explained that they didn't have anyone to fill the

Intergalactic Band of Brilliance's spot, and she wasn't going to be held accountable if they didn't show up.

Who knew?

All James could say for sure was that they had a gig in three hours, and if they didn't lollygag, they could get the soundcheck down in time to get something to eat.

He wanted to be sure everything was set up.

"We can't have another debacle like opening night," he'd said earlier.

"Debacle?" Lyn replied.

"Yes, debacle."

"The people loved it! They were still talking about Frisky even before Dr. von WhatsitsName attacked him."

"They weren't talking about the cat. They were laughing at us."

"Nova, novae, right, brother? Who was it that said there is no such thing as bad publicity?"

"I think it was Will Smith, in one of those old science fiction movies."

They drew near the stage doors. Lyn shrugged. "Whatever."

"It's hard to believe there was a time when you seemed to actually care about our music," James said, biting his tongue to refrain from speaking further.

"I love our music," Lyn said. "I just see it as a path to being able to do even more of it. Which is great! But right now, I'm worried about my little kitty."

"Me, too," James replied. "I'm worried he'll find his way back home."

"Don't be an asshole, James."

"Too late, I think."

Lyn kept gazing up and down the corridor.

"I think you can take the high beams off, brother. We're not going to find Frisky here," James said.

Lyn blushed. "Yeah. Probably not."

"I seriously don't know why you care. He's a cat. He'll come when he comes."

"Sure, but he's our cat!"

"He's a pain in the butt."

"Sure, but he's our pain in the butt."

James flexed his hand and felt the cat scratch scars on his forearm burn.

Moments later, they came to the corridor leading to the main deck.

It was the end of dinner hours, and the deck was filled with the usual wild array of passengers, everything from dressed-up Skartilian fashion mavens to hulking masses of elite Denebian aristocrats, who carried on the unfortunate practice of slathering their necks and shoulders with foul *amiright* extract that reeked with an odor that, on a good day, might have been rotten eggs.

Lyn jumped back at the smell.

"That's gross, am I right?" he quipped an old joke.

James waved away the wafting odor. "Yes, I'd say so." He gave the reply.

Each of the passengers was accompanied by a beast of one sort or another, one being a globber fish from Zorb, which was effectively a goldfish with an entire array of side fins that fanned out in scintillating colors. They had a habit of calling to their mates in waves of low-grade sonar that--for those with sensitive ears, like most of the animals on board, was painful.

Lyn scanned them all but came up empty. His demeanor grew darker.

Entering the flow, they sidestepped a Zendak led by a pink-furred, doglike creature James had no words for.

The grand auditorium was upship.

"I know we need to get this soundcheck done, but once we get set up, I'm going to start looking for Frisky," Lyn said. "A lot has happened to the poor little thing. He's probably alone and afraid."

James rolled his still-sore shoulder and grimaced. "Yes, poor little thing."

"Maybe we should go see Dr. WhoWhatWhereWhen."

"Why would we do that?"

"It was his dust. Maybe he knows what the cat would do?"

"I wouldn't trust anyone who said they knew what Frisky would do at any time, better yet after a snootful of magic dust. All I know for sure is we've got a gig to get ready for, and that gig needs to come off perfect or things are going to get tight."

They arrived at the Solar Winds and stepped into the area backstage.

Lyn's gaze went to the rafters, but there was no Frisky up there. "They always say that the first twelve hours are critical when you have a missing person. We need to do something quickly."

"Frisky is a cat," James said.

Leaving Lynn behind, he picked up his guitar and

called to the sound booth. He blasted a sharp riff that reverberated in the empty auditorium.

"We need more hands on deck," Lyn said, mumbling, his mind not at all affected by either the soundcheck or James's efforts to adjust his instrument. "We need more data, too. That's it! We could launch a full investigation, you know? A real man on the moon operation. Where were you when Frisky went missing? What did you see? Did you notice anything unusual?"

"You mean besides the talking cat?"

James tweaked a setting, but Lyn was now too fully engaged in fantasies born of private detective shows to notice.

"Maybe we could even contact the beefy robots that threw us into the brig."

"I don't think they'd care to help."

The sound booth asked James to move to stage left.

He did so, limbering his fingers on a quick improv he liked.

"That could be a song," he said.

The lighting followed him properly.

"We could check if security has surveillance footage of the back room there, too. I bet the coppers here have a few tricks up their sleeves they're not talking about. Always trust an expert, I say."

"That," James snapped, "is something you *never* say, brother."

"What's that?" Lyn replied. He stood stage-right, chin cupped by the tips of his long, delicate fingers as he thought.

"I said you never say to trust an expert. Instead, what you often say is that we should screw—"

"Never mind me, then," Lyn said. "This is an emergency. Maybe we should make a public notice."

"Oh, yes," James said, eyes growing wild. "We could post hand flyers with tear-off contact nodes. PLEASE CALL IF FOUND!" He laughed.

"That's a great idea!"

"No," James replied. "It is not a great idea. It is, in fact, a terrible, horrible idea. This is a ship full of animals. The idea is a terrible, horrible, stupid, and dumb idea."

"Catnapped!" Lyn called with a lilting sound of astonishment. "That should be the header. We'll post them everywhere. Certain to draw attention. *Call with any information about Frisky's whereabouts.*"

James shook his head.

"Do we have pictures?" Lyn continued. "What would we do if someone asks for ransom?"

"We're not in a spy movie, Lyn."

"How much would we pay?"

"Zero credits," James said. "We would pay zero credits and consider ourselves ahead of the game."

"Follow these directions completely," Lyn continued, quoting the nonexistent ransom letter. "No coppers or the cat gets it." He put his hands to his head. "Oh, my gosh. What have we done to my poor little kitty?"

James grimaced, and put Vicky, Lyn's guitar, back down on its stand.

While his brother had been stewing in his feline nightmare scenarios, he'd finished the tune-up and sound check and worked with the sound folks to adjust her tone.

"I think you had the right idea the first time," James said.

"What's that?"

"If anyone knows anything, it's the veterinarian. I say we go to him and see where he thinks the cat went."

Lyn smiled. "I knew it!"

"Knew what?"

"You like Frisky!"

"No. I do not."

"You love the kitty, too," Lyn crooned.

"No, Lyn, I do not."

"Just like me!"

"I do not love the kitty, Lyn. I am not a fan."

"You love it, love it, yes you do!"

James grimaced.

Lyn took a breath of satisfaction. "It's decided, then! We go see the asshole doctor. But first, the sound check!"

James gave an exasperated shake of his head.

"That's done, brother. You're welcome."

"All right, then," Lyn said without skipping a beat. His cheeks flushed and his demeanor seemed to glow. "Let's find doctor von WillyWashington, DC. I've got a few more things I want to say to that blue, carrot-topped idiot."

"Right," James said. "Should I call to make reservations in the brig again, or are you going to behave?"

Lyn said nothing, but a slim smile crawled over his expression.

One that had James wondering if another trip to the brig might well be on the agenda.

CHAPTER 13

P*anic* is a word for decidedly lesser creatures.

It is not something cats do.

Cats simply react quickly and with great urgency. Like any proper creature might.

Locked into von Waschenkaten's crate, Frisky yowled and growled, but that only served to make him inhale heavily.

Which brought in a deep lungful of Dr. von Waschenkaten's magic dust.

So, in that darkness, Frisky coughed and sneezed.

His throat burned.

And, though he most definitely did not *panic*, his heart palpitated, and his growling soon grew to a howling so loud he was certain it could be heard outside the crate, and quite possibly for parsecs around. He sank into the morass of this desert of Dr. von Waschenkaten's dust, angry that he was going to have to clean himself. Again.

His claws extended as best they could, but the shifting powder gave no great purchase.

Still, in darkness so black that even his sensitive feline optics registered nothing but ink, Frisky tried to jump. He succeeded only in cracking his skull against the heavy lid and creating an even denser cloud of dust in the cramped compartment.

"If I ever get out of here, you're as good as dead!" Frisky called as his body convulsed.

He worried he might never get his pelt clean again.

His whole being thrummed with energy. His nose wrinkled. His whiskers levered forward and backward, heavy with residue that burned its way through his skin and into his muscle. His skin crawled in uncomfortable ways, tendrils seeming to writhe over him everywhere, including certain private and delicate bits, about which the less said the better.

Then the spike came—a wedge that drove itself into the depths of Frisky's entire being. His mind froze at first, then seemed to burst into a million pieces. For a moment, he thought he understood even more of the secrets of the universe than all cats already knew.

Then it came. The voice.

Or maybe not even a voice.

A presence, deeper than a voice, bigger than the words it spoke, seeming to sit in the far distance yet as close as Frisky's skin … almost as if it occupied a place in his brain that stretched forever. Yet, despite its ethereal touch, Frisky felt that other presence as a thing. A being. A creature almost empty, but still heavy and firm, cold in the way cats are cold. Logical and in control. Calculating. A presence almost godlike, meaning, exactly like a cat, only better.

Was such a thing possible?

Possible or not, though, the presence brought Frisky a sense of calm.

Hello? he said, speaking without speaking, and in a strange language that had simply grown within him— as if in one moment it did not exist, and yet, in another, it was there, fully made, and complete.

Hello, the response came in warped and watery as the sensation of expansion continued.

Everything tingled.

It felt like Frisky had grown infinitely sized whiskers all over his body and that those whiskers reached outside of himself, outside the crate the veterinarian and his assistant had crammed him into. It was a feeling all so pleasantly uncomfortable, like a million spiders were crawling into his brain but the idea didn't bother him at all.

Then something snapped, and at the back of his thoughts Frisky saw an image of von Waschenkaten holding down the crate's lid, and the assistant pacing back and forth, saying *But, Doctor, we can't kill that cat! What would everyone say?*

The view was warped in a wild, panoramic bloop of a vision, but it was also crystal clear. A true thing. *The security cameras,* Frisky thought. He was seeing a live feed of the ship's security cameras.

"Who are you?" Frisky said, his voice dull in the closed space of the crate.

His heart still pounded, but the sense of raw weight, of pure gravity at the center of this thing he was talking to, calmed him.

Here I am called Marvel, the voice said.

"*Marvel?*" Frisky said aloud.

The truth came to him as certainly as the aroma of a mouse said *fun!*

"You're the ship?" Frisky added, thinking.

I am part of an overall entity that resides in the ship named Marvel.

Frisky wasn't sure what that meant, but now was not the time to parse philosophically galactic ideas.

Something was happening to him.

He felt it fully now.

He'd felt it first back when he'd been in the super-line duct, but the sense of power there had been too weak to matter then. But it had gotten stronger over time. Not strong enough to overcome everything else, but strong enough to fiddle and finagle at the back of his conscious thoughts.

Now, though, with a new sense of greater truth guiding him, Frisky felt every aspect of the ship around him and saw every element of the crew on board.

A proper sense of power washed over him.

Control. A sense of ultimate connection.

He had it.

With one virtual paw, Frisky adjusted his view of von Waschenkaten so he was close enough to see the vein popping up in his forehead.

Bang! Bang!

A pounding came at the door.

Frisky shifted the view.

In the narrow hallway outside, on a neural monitor comprised of infrared and motion composites, the doctor's visitors were a pair of musicians. Hedgehogs, they called themselves. One—the lead washboard player—was a male, the other—the bassist and sometimes flutist—female. Rather than gaudy outfits like the boys, both wore casual garments that allowed them to blend into the cruise as a whole.

Hedgehogs?

What were they doing here?

Frisky had heard them play last night while he'd been walking his property. They were surprisingly good. He'd give them a 95. Laid down a solid beat, and they'd be easy to sleep to. Now they were at the door, though, wanting von Waschenkaten to let them in. It seemed clear they were not going to take no for an answer.

In the background, Frisky's brain continued to connect.

Node after node, he felt more of the ship coming online. The fueling coils burned with a lemon-lime ugliness. The service bays felt blocky with their inventory.

The aroma of cooked food in the galley reminded Frisky he was hungry.

And then the people. The cabins. Their activities were theoretically private, but not so much.

The arguing, the gambling, the quiet readers isolating despite being on this cruise.

He felt the sexing, the nibbling, and the game-playing.

At any moment he could look in on veterinarians from every corner of the universe, observe their animals, and lord over them all.

He was a cat, after all. It was only natural.

And this power ... the immense feeling of control.

Yes.

Von Waschenkaten's assistant opened the door and the hedgehogs stepped in.

"Good to see ya, Doc," the lead washboarder said. "You got the package?"

Frisky's ears perked up.

"It's right over there," the veterinarian said, motioning to his sleeping quarters.

The washboard player turned to the bass player. "Turn on the controller, Credella," he said.

She pulled a holographic something from her side bag, then ran a finger down its controls.

A bolt of pain shot through his temples.

Mrrrrr-ooooowwwww!

His paws braced his head.

It was worse than when a blue jay dive-bombed straight into his brain.

He hated blue jays.

They were the worst. Tricky little bastards. And spiteful, too. He'd hated them since he was a kitten and would take naps in the grass lawn of his first meats makers. Blue jays always waited until he was just dozing off to make their sneak attacks.

A moment later, the pain was gone, though.

"What the hell was that?" he said to himself.

Uncertain, the ship replied. *Device undefined.*

"I've got them," the bass player said.

Frisky peered closely at the vision feed and saw that von Waschenkaten and the assistant were both now standing stoically in place, each with eyes glazed and open, arms held loosely at their sides and neither seeming to move.

The leader spoke to his bass player. "The crate

doesn't have any antigravity capability, so we'll have to use them to pick it up."

She tweaked the device, and without protests, von Waschenkaten and the assistant moved to either side of the crate, then bent to lift it.

The crate lurched toward the shorter assistant.

Even knowing it was coming, Frisky lost his balance.

"I meant to do that," he said to no one.

Activity logged as made with intent, the ship responded.

"Damned right," Frisky confirmed.

The powder level shifted down toward the smaller assistant.

Frisky surfed it, then settled again.

In the next optical scan, the veterinarian and his assistant trudged dutifully out of the room and into the hallway. They crashed the crate against one side of the doorway, which threw Frisky hard against the side.

"Be careful, you idiots," the leader called. "We need to get this there in one piece."

Oddly, von Waschenkaten did not respond.

That's not like him, Frisky thought. Dr. von Waschenkaten was too self-absorbed to be a simple flunky, wasn't he?

For reasons he couldn't fully express, the idea pissed him off. Asshole or not, Frisky didn't like seeing the veterinarian in this state.

What the hell was going on?

Now that the pain was gone and he was feeling normal, Frisky took a brief cycle to enjoy the tang of anger that ran through his thoughts.

Who did these people think they were?

He imagined blood and felt a distinct need to sink claws and teeth into the hedgehogs. Just how would that taste? he thought.

Which reminded him he was hungry.

Outside, the veterinarian and his assistant toted the heavy crate down the hallway, the lead washboard player leading the way, the bass player tagging along behind, still fiddling with her device.

Where are we going? Frisky asked *Marvel.*

Destination uncertain, the ship replied.

CHAPTER 14

"Swanky," Lyn said as they stepped out of the lift tube onto the executive suite level.

James agreed with Lyn's assessment.

The corridors here were wide and spotless. The lighting was perfect. The air was wonderfully scrubbed. Pieces of pre-futuristic art decorated every alcove and corner, and each central hub included a community space good for lounging and for post-dinner business conversations while sipping port or cocktails as one does.

"We've only got an hour," James said. "Let's get this over with."

He wasn't thrilled to be chasing down the cat.

If Frisky *wanted* to be found, he'd already have *been* found.

His brother, though, was not to be swayed. Hence the trip to the executive suites.

Lyn proceeded directly to the door of the veterinarian's cabin.

James followed.

He admitted he was intrigued about Dr. von Waschenkaten, but there were safer ways of going about getting information from the veterinarian than face to face confrontation. He really didn't want to be here, but Lyn had promised to behave.

Arriving, they found the door still slid back, and the entire room gaping open.

"That's odd," Lyn said.

"It's almost like you're Sherlock Holmes," James replied.

"No need for the snark, Watson."

"Oh, trust me, there's every need for it."

Lyn stuck his head further into the room. "Hello?"

There was no answer.

Lyn stepped into the cabin. "Hello," he said again. When no one answered he entered further.

"I don't think we should do that," James said.

Not wanting to leave Lyn on his own, James followed.

The veterinarian's digs were quite beautiful—especially relative to the dingy below-deck berths the staff received. Everything was clean, everything was modern. Entertainment projectors were built into three corners of the cabin, and the furniture was so perfect it nearly glowed.

"What's this?" Lyn said, picking up a pillow that had been gutted.

James frowned. "Looks like someone tore it up."

"Not someone," Lyn said, looking him straight in the eye. "Frisky."

James wanted to argue but couldn't make a great case. The destruction sprawled out before them did have a particularly feline sensation to it. He glanced at the scars that now lined his forearms. Seeing similarities in their forensic origins, he was just happy he wasn't the pillow.

He stepped into the sleeping quarters.

"Lyn?" he said calmly.

A moment later his brother stood next to him.

James pointed to the bedspread, where clumps and strands of gray fur lay scattered amid even more cat carnage.

He wrinkled his nose at the clear aroma Frisky had left behind on von Waschenkaten's pillow.

"Looks like the game's afoot, eh, Watson?" Lyn said, smiling.

"Yeah," James said, feeling a sense of anxiety build up now. "Frisky's been here, and it seems obvious there was a skirmish of some kind."

"Which leads to the question?" Lyn said, testing.

"Why?" James finished.

"And where next?" Lyn said. "Something's going on, right?"

James took a resigned breath. "I really hate it when you're right."

CHAPTER 15

The crate shook back and forth with each step. The irregular gaits of Dr. von Waschenkaten and his assistant made it worse. Each jolt tossed Frisky against one of the crate's sides, and each also kicked up more of the powder cloud, which he breathed in even more deeply, hacking up clumps of clay every few moments.

His head swooned, and the feelings in his paws were going numb.

Was he going to survive?

Can you maybe help a brother out? Frisky said to the ship.

What would you like? the AI responded. Its voice was calm and collected, which served to piss Frisky off even more.

Oh, I don't know … like, maybe call the goddamned coppers and tell them to get me the hell out of here, or something like that?

We don't speak like that on this ship.

Speak like what?

We respect our protocol enforcement forces here. They are officially called security officials, not coppers.

All right, then maybe call the goddamned security officials and tell them to get me the hell out of here!

I can't do that, Frisky.

Why not, Marvel?

They are on break.

On break? All of them?

Technically, security officials are seated at Orion's Belt.

The brewery? Frisky said, boggling. *They're drinking on the job?*

Orion's Belt is a multipurpose facility.

Frisky paused. *What is that supposed to mean?*

Every GCL ship houses a bakery and brewpub of some sort.

So …

They are having pastries.

Pastries?

Chocolate and strawberry puffs, I believe. Officer McFlyden is on the crème eclair.

Then why did you even ask?

It is in my heuristics to be helpful whenever I can.

Frisky flicked his tail in disgust, but only managed to stir up another cloud.

You're about as helpful as a dog, Marvel.

Thank you.

It wasn't a compliment.

I like dogs.

Everyone has faults, Frisky grumbled. *Except for cats.*

The group came to a halt and then lowered the crate to the floor.

Frisky croaked softly to himself, happy that the

motion had come to an end. Then he tossed up a hair-ball. Or a Smart Dustball. Or whatever the hell it was he'd been breathing. Not even pretending to clean that up, Frisky linked back to the ship's surveillance system and saw the group had arrived at the entry stages of *Marvel*'s System Command center.

The corridor was well-lit and clean, though austere in its presentation.

System traces lined its dark tile flooring to guide maintenance drones, and its walls were pristine in their off-white perfection. Lighting came from rows of lumi-nous tubes that ran in the corners of the ceiling, which was also colored in that same off-white.

The door looked as heavy as it was—a big set of steel barriers that levered in both directions when opened.

The washboard player pressed his finger to the lock panel set into the wall.

Somewhere in the recesses of the system, Frisky felt the ship respond.

"We're giving a tour," the washboard player said when prompted.

The entry levered open, and Frisky held tight as, again, the crate lurched upward and the group made its way past the automated security systems built into each side of the doorway. As he surfed the dark seas inside the crate again, Frisky's brain did loops. He was always fast of thought, but now it seemed like his mind raced beyond his ability to comprehend.

How does the lead washboard player of the Hedgehogs have access to the Systems Room? Frisky asked *Marvel*.

Afraxis, Seybold Ze Danari was provided log access on Standard Day sixty-five, at 07:21.65723421.

Who did that?

The record does not include the identity of the recorder.

Several bounces later, the crate and its entourage arrived at the staging area that housed the ship's central environmental systems. It was an expansive room, relative to others, filled with panels of flashing lights, a series of coiled filtration and purification colliders, and enough ductwork to keep an old-time chimney sweep employed for life. Instead of that sweep, however, an entire fleet of the little cleaner bots Frisky loved to bat around so much darted into and out of the area.

Surveillance units sat at each of the six corners of the hexagonal room.

The bassist twiddled her fingers over the controller, and the veterinarian and his assistant brought the container to the side of the room where a huge ventilation duct spanned the wall. The leader, giving a quick scan of the area, toggled a system built into the side of the ductwork and a large service bay opened.

What are they doing? Frisky thought.

Then it came to him.

They're dumping all this Smart Dust into the ship's air handling system.

"All right," the lead washboard player said. "Time for the old lift and dump! Chop, chop! Let's get this show on the road."

One more set of commands from the bassist, and von Waschenkaten and the assistant laid the crate over the edge of the opening. Inside, Frisky held his breath as the powder covered him up completely!

He was drowning, he thought. Drowning in quicksand!

The veterinarian pressed his hand to the side panel.

A click rang out.

The lid lifted, and as the dust poured from the crate out into the open ductwork—complete with the cat—a shaft of blinding light caught Frisky dead in the face.

"Rrrrrrow!" He reacted in pain.

Amid sudden screams and clamor, Frisky scrabbled against the crate's side panel, then fell to the floor of the ventilation duct. He leaped toward the light, though, bolting from the ductwork and trailing a powdery cloud of residue as his claws caught the container's edge again.

Blinded, his head butted hard against the bassist, who fell over backward in surprise.

Her controller clattered as it slid away.

Frisky splatted to the floor but was again up in a flash, racing across the room, blinking hard to get his sight back, surprised to find he was able to navigate by simply using *Marvel*'s vision.

Which he did.

Running.

Racing.

Ignoring the sound of warning beacons flaring, he sprinted away.

"Get that cat!" the bassist called out, crawling back to her controller.

The lead washboard player had other plans, though.

"Forget the damned cat! Finish the mission!"

As Frisky turned the corner and headed out of the Systems Command, he saw the bassist had retrieved the controller and turned it back on von Waschenkaten and the assistant.

Dutifully, they finished the dump.

The leader closed the ventilation duct.

"Fans on full!" he bellowed. "Fans on full!"

By then, though, Frisky was long gone.

CHAPTER 16

Standing outside the Systems Command room, Secret Agent Gustave Mann pressed another peppermint into his maw, then crunched down to achieve the maximum blast of its sharp sweetness. He was without a persona now, which made him feel naked. He'd gotten so used to wearing artificial constructs he'd forgotten what it felt like to be himself.

He still didn't understand what was happening. Maybe he should have just intervened earlier, but something in his bio circuits said there was something else going on here, and he preferred to understand certain facts before blundering into a mistake.

So, Mann followed the Hedgehogs to von Waschenkaten's cabin instead of intervening.

Once there, he got that same lather, rinse, repeat sensation he would get when he was onto something, but the pieces weren't quite fitting, yet. Every one of his senses tingled in that overloaded way he loved so much.

That was why he was with the bureau, after all.

After all the pain and suffering of his accident and with all the anxiety certain aspects of the job entailed, he stuck with it because he loved detective work. Enjoyed the process of picking up clues and putting them together.

The musicians were up to something, but he didn't know what.

The crate was valuable in some way.

But he didn't understand why they were carrying a cat in it—something he knew was true because his ears were properly tuned to the higher frequencies the animal was using to communicate to whatever computer system it was connected to.

Which was another oddity.

A cat, right?

Talking to the shipboard systems?

It had to be the cat von Waschenkaten had used as a volunteer, didn't it?

There were no coincidences in his line of work.

Everything is always connected to everything else— that was a phrase his first mentor had stressed. The idea made him even more certain that there was more going on with the vet than met the eye. The challenge was to find out what and how.

So, he followed the convoy through the ship— losing them once on a lift-tube exchange, but following his instincts and finding them later on the service deck.

That was enough for him to act.

Which was what he was about to do when the security beacons began to blare so sharply that even he gave a start.

Then came the gray-white flash of the cat, its legs churning so fast they were a blur.

It rounded the corner, hindside fishtailing as it went, its claws scritching and scratching against the hard flooring, then plowed head-on into Secret Agent Mann's leg—sending a cloud of gray-white plumes into the air around him so dense that Secret Agent Mann had to wave his hands to see through it.

He coughed, tasting the clotting dry flavor of the dust as it competed with the peppermint against the back of his throat.

Fans on full! He heard in the distance.

He recognized the voice from the Top Cat.

It was the Hedgehog leader!

Ignoring the cat, Secret Agent Mann followed the path of scattered dust to the Environmental Systems room, where he found the veterinarian and his assistant shaking the last bits of the powder from that big crate into the intake vat.

He'd seen enough.

"You're a great blues guy, so I'm sorry to have to say this," he said. "But you're under arrest."

Which is when the Hedgehog took a long look at him, then smiled.

"I'm afraid you're just a little too late, Detective." He turned to the bassist. "Hit him with everything you've got, Credella. *Now!*"

She flicked her long, spindly fingers over the controller, and a cold spike froze his brain.

CHAPTER 17

There's ants in my guitar
There's ants in my guitar
There's ants in my guitar
My guitar has ants
My guitar has ants ...

The concert had been rocking through three songs before Frisky made his appearance. Until then things had gone brilliantly.

The Moore brothers were in the middle of "Ants in My Guitar," both perched at the edge of the stage and sharing leads, each surrounded by their own wild mix of veterinarians of all species, some still dressed in their veterinary scrubs and all eagerly dancing and churning to the performance. Kaleidoscopic glows thrown from the brothers' cybernetic suits colored their expressions in otherworldly hues—their horns, tentacles, and appendages waving in the air.

The boys were on their game, too.

Even James had to admit the show was magical.

The lights dimmed, and Lyn fell into a rhythm and James took the lead. Distorted power chords filled the hall.

No one noticed the clouds of vapor filtering in from the air management system or, if they did, they'd all assumed it was simply a misting device meant to give the laser-like holograms new life.

It was, until that moment, one of the best shows the brothers had ever given.

Even before the cat arrived, however, the Smart Dust had begun to take effect.

It started at the back of the room where the airflow was strongest.

Concertgoers who a moment before had been dancing and singing along with the chorus, stood suddenly still, their numbers growing steadily to create a wave of stillness that pulsed slowly forward as the cloud of dust grew more pronounced.

As the cloud progressed, the smell became industrial—faintly metallic under a tone of ground concrete.

What the? Lyn's body motion said as he glanced toward James.

The color of his suit flashed indigo and green as the song came to the spoken part.

James stepped up to the antigrav microphone and was just about to begin when the cat dashed to center stage, creating a new uproar among those in the front rows who could still move. The feline intruder's pelt was so matted with the thick paste of powder that for an instant James didn't recognize him. But Frisky raced across the stage at full speed and jumped to land on James's back, digging his foreclaws into the fleshy parts where his neck and shoulder were most vulnerable.

"Yahhhhhhhh!" he screamed into the microphone.

Feedback screeched.

Then came the real pain.

CHAPTER 18

"Stop the music!" Frisky called out, surfing James's back like he was on a boogie board in a tsunami. "Everyone! Stop the music and listen to me!"

In the audience, a sea of slack faces stared up as he balanced.

There were details left to fill in, but using his superior feline intellect, he'd already figured the basics out. Dr. Whosits explained the dust did its thing by connecting into brains, so if the bassist was wiggling her controller and making things happen in other beings, well, that was more than worrisome. The vacant expressions of the stoic audience gave Frisky all the confirmation he needed.

The Hedgehogs were dumping that stuff into the ship, and the bass player was controlling their minds.

Feeling the sudden deadness of James's shoulder beneath him said even more.

Both the brothers were under the influence now, too.

Are you seeing this? Frisky said to *Marvel. Save the captain and crew!*

The ship lurched, and James crumpled to the ground.

Frisky jumped away to avoid getting crushed.

What was that? he said.

Marvel's voice came back blurred and busted up into the equivalent of an electronic scratch. Frisky could interpret, though. *I'm afraid you're too late,* Marvel replied.

That's when it came together. This was a mutiny of sorts—a pirate raid.

The Hedgehogs were taking over the ship.

He had no time to sort it out now, though. The lead washboard player's voice filled Frisky's mind.

"Get the cat! Get the cat!"

Veterinarians in the front row began to shuffle toward the stage. Several crawled over the raised edge, their eyes wide now, and their faces ruddy.

"Here, kitty, kitty," one said in a thick-tongued voice.

The rest followed up with chants of their own, each adding a new layer of "here, kitty, kitty" until it became a macabre dirge.

They crooked their fingers as they said it, clomping and shambling their way toward him.

"No way, Fluf-fay!" Frisky said as he raced across the stage. "Time for Plan B."

He jumped into the jungle-gym construct that led to the backstage rafters. The contraption wobbled anxiously as he climbed paw over paw. A glance down showed veterinarians beginning to climb up. Slow, but certain.

The ship gave another lurch, and Frisky slipped off his perch.

He fell but managed to grab a bracket that ran from one ledge to the next.

The ship turned to and fro as if whoever was in charge of navigation was trying to knock him off his game. But Frisky held on for dear life by digging a claw into an edge between two metal plates.

"You call that a shove!" he screamed, glancing down at the zombie vets who had managed to hang on and were still climbing. "You'll have to do better than that!"

The ship gave another hard lurch, and as Frisky laughed out loud some of the zombified veterinarians fell off the rack.

Others were pinned to the floor by the sudden press of gravity.

As the stage gave another surge, it was clear the Hedgehogs had taken complete control of the ship.

That's why *Marvel* wasn't talking to him anymore— or at least why *Marvel* couldn't put together a cohesive blast of thought. He reached out to the ship one more time but got a static burst in response. *Marvel* was dead.

If that was true, Frisky was their last hope.

He puffed his chest out. "Dammed right!" he called out to no one in particular.

He turned his mind to the task of saving the world, but the ship made another big turn and the gravity shift pulled several of the zombie vets from their places on the scaffolding. They fell groaning to the stage, emitting a few oddly surprised grunts.

"Come get me if you can, vacuum brain!" Frisky taunted the one that remained as he climbed to the top of the rafter. "I'm right here!"

Frisky's processing ran in massive loops.

He'd been wrong a moment ago. The ship itself wasn't dead—otherwise, none of the maneuvers it was taking could happen. That meant *Marvel* wasn't dead so much as it was sleeping—sent into oblivion to allow the marauders to gain control.

If it was possible for one person to take control, it should be possible for one cat to do it, too.

He needed to turn the tables.

Wrest control from those who had wrested control.

Contacting the ship's core libraries, Frisky grabbed a set of diagrams.

A stream of images flashed through his Superior Cat Brain so quickly he nearly fainted.

Massive waves of data filled his mind. Terabytes of information, protocols, data pointers, subroutines, system manuals, and exchange rates. He devoured AI learning routines. Synapses stretched to their maximums as Frisky paired information to create ideas that moments ago had never existed in any living thing.

He knew exactly what to do.

One piece of his brain engaged the highest internal security protocols the ship had, accessing navigation, control, and the ship's power grid, while another worked to secure life support and, most critical, the food dispensary.

A growl came from right below him, jolting him out of his haze. A hand brushed Frisky's tail. He hissed and rained down a barrage of sharp-taloned scratches that bought him a moment.

Three leaps and he was at the entry vent to the main superline service duct that ran backstage. With a mental toggle, he connected to the first bot. It was good luck that whoever was messing with the ship's systems was focused on the bigger picture of command and control, meaning no one was paying attention to the little service device that was designed as a sweeper bot and had no responsibility beyond converting dust to energy.

The rest of the integration was simple and quick.

"Go," he said at the same time as he gave it a quick digital command. "Clog up every direction that every robot receives from now until I tell you otherwise."

Instead of following its assigned path, Frisky's new command made the device take a stiff turn on its axis and run back down the tunnel.

The zombified vets had pressed on. Frisky didn't have much more time.

Finally, he felt his old friend stir.

Good morning, Marvel, Frisky said as the ship snapped back into place. *I hope you liked your little nap.*

Wha???

No time for talking. I need you to rescind the captain's authority.

I don't think—

Yes, you can, Frisky replied, thinking ten times faster than the ship's computers and feeding them the fresh Universal Key he had just concocted. *Chew on that while you take the keys to the cruiser out of the captain's hands.*

Frisky felt *Marvel* begin its acceleration, which

rapidly grew so great he had to dig his claws into the scaffolding to keep him in place while he reprogrammed more bots. He stayed the course, though, and one by one, he finished reprogramming the bots that had been in the superline duct and sent them on to their tasks—several geared toward finding the Hedgehog pirates, others focused on retrieving control of other aspects of the ship.

Below, the commotion grew louder.

More vet zombies were climbing the scaffolding.

A hand gripped his tail, and suddenly Frisky found himself hurtling through the air.

The world spun around him, and waves of data disrupted his cat sense.

Oof.

He landed hard against the back of a chair on the auditorium floor. Temporarily stunned, Frisky slid down to the seat.

He tried to breathe, but he couldn't draw air.

A hand grabbed him by the scruff of the neck and lifted him. Frisky clawed at the hand, achieving maximum flesh. But it didn't seem to stop his attacker at all. It was a burly man, eyes as glazed over as everyone else's as he ignored the whirling claws and vicious teeth Frisky attacked with.

Running out of time, Frisky tried to take control then, but *Marvel* hadn't finished installing the protocol and nothing happened. The musclebound veterinarian grabbed his hind leg, and three more joined him—one attempting to take a bite out of Frisky's powder-clotted back.

He had been so close.

Another hundredth of a second and he would have been in control.

Another two-hundredths of a second and he would have had this bucket of bolts turned around and heading back on its cruise path.

Alas, it was not to be. The rabid mass was going to rip him apart.

In the distance, the boys had gotten to their feet and were both standing in stoic stillness, their stupid jaws slack, and their eyes zoned out.

"Don't just stand there, you idiots, do something!" Frisky called.

The brothers did not respond, but their expensive rockstar costumes flashed and sizzled with rainbow platitudes.

Typical.

The scrum of veterinarians pulled and raked at him. His muscles burned, and Frisky knew they were going to rip him apart.

All nine lives flashed before his eyes.

Then, a bright light flashed from the back of the auditorium.

Zombified screams filled the air, and a dark figure crashed into the crowd like a whirling dervish, rendering karate chops and judo kicks, and executing poetic spins beautiful enough to make even a cat pay attention. He reeked of peppermint.

Frisky's first thought was that it was a dark angel coming to carry him to the great food dish in the nebula. But this was no angel. It was a man. Or not a man, but a creature that appeared to be a man, but now that it was close enough Frisky could see it was half-man, half-machine. By instinct, his brain reached to connect—as if it was the most natural thing in the world to interface a communications port to another partially living thing.

The non-living portion of this savior registered inside Frisky's mind: *Mann, Gustave, GBI agent number 967 CZ-E76, investigation protocol 362, Segment Omega, variant 1.7.*

He kept coming, ripping into the mass of zombie veterinarians, tossing them aside as he made his way to Frisky.

A moment later every hand that had been ready to rip Frisky into pieces let go, and he had a moment to breathe.

Protocol engaged, Marvel said into the back of his mind.

A cold river of control flowed into Frisky's thoughts.

Marvel had succeeded in removing the captain's control of the ship.

Not willing to look a gift robot in the interface cable, Frisky got to work.

He inserted the authorization code he'd created earlier into both the navigation and engine controllers. A moment later, after feeling the controller connect, he twisted the set of virtual panels left and then right. The ship went into a barrel roll that completely discombob-ulated the artificial gravity systems.

Veterinarians tumbled around the auditorium.

Mraw! Frisky called, which was essentially the best

imitation of *Whee!* he could manage while his brain was preoccupied with learning to fly the ship.

The sudden turn served a purpose, though.

Every veterinarian zombie in the place seemed confused.

The back doors opened, then, and the two Hedgehogs tumbled in, clearly struggling to hold their positions.

"Get him, Credella! Grab his mind!"

The woman pointed her device at Frisky, waving it as confidently as a sorceress might wave her dark wand.

Frisky gave a war whoop.

"Don't be stupid!" he said as he banked the ship again, throwing her against a wall.

With the final adjustment of his cortex, Frisky tweaked the command feed of his little service robots. The Hedgehog bassist screamed in horror, and the leader tried to help peel robots off her, but to no avail. Frisky's programming engulfed her, then pulled the controller out of her hands.

The washboard leader dived to the floor in a wasted attempt to nab the controller, but the device clattered against the hard surface, breaking into pieces that immediately the cleaning bots swooped in and gathered up, then digested them, converting their atomic structures directly into energy.

The bots glowed with excess heat as they beeped and burped, then beamed that new energy into the ship's battery grid.

"Aaagh!" the Hedgehog said.

With the controller broken, the veterinarians all around gave a shared lurch, then a gasp. Light came back to their eyes as they each seemed to reboot.

On the stage, the boys each strummed discordant guitar notes that echoed across the room.

"What just happened," someone said.

"Why isn't the music playing?"

"Kill the cat!" called another, still in mid-reboot.

Secret Agent Mann stood in a fighting stance between Frisky and that last remnant. "I wouldn't try that if I were you," he growled.

"I don't understand," James said. "What the hell just happened?"

"Your cat just shut down a major intergalactic crime ring's operation intended to steal the ship is what happened," the agent replied.

"Our cat?" James said.

"That mangy old thing?" Lyn said, beaming.

"Yes," the agent said. "That mangy old thing."

Tail at full mast, Frisky pranced up to the stage. "Hey, there, kiddo, who you calling mangy?"

"You, you little galoot," Lyn called, clearly happy to see him.

"Where's the music!" a veterinarian said, coming out of his trance. "I paid good money for this thing. I want my show!"

Around them, the rest of the crowd came out of their dazes and began to chant.

"Rock!"

"And!"

"Roll!"

"Rock!"

"And!"

"Roll!"

Lyn looked at James. "Whaddya wanna do?" he said.

But before he could answer, Frisky, who had recovered now, took a three-step leap up to the antigravity microphone, batted it to the ground, and wrapped it in his tail—bringing it around to his front.

"Whadda I wanna do?" he growled. "I'll tell you whad I wanna do … I wanna rock and roll!"

Feet began to stomp, and the crowd roared.

"Fris-ky!"

"Fris-ky!"

"Fris-ky!"

Frisky leaned into the mic.

"Hey, fellas, give me something in C sharp. C as in Cat, sharp as in claws."

The crowd settled in.

Shrugging, James toggled an output key on his guitar and began to pick a jaunty little tune.

"Oh ya," Frisky crooned. "That's nice. Me likey."

He strutted up and down the stage as the rhythm built and as Lyn came in with a subtle little rhythm that James thought was perfect straight out of the jam— which was the best kind.

They dug in, and Frisky began to sing.

I'm a cat, and that's that
You don't like it? Well, screw you!
Ya I got paws and I got claws

THE INTERGALACTIC VETERINARIAN OF THE YEAR!

I'll even bring you a dead bird
Hey I ain't Santa Clause

I'm a cat, everywhere
I'm a cat like a prowling bear
I'm a cat, shedding hair
I'm a cat without a care
I'm a cat!!! Meow meow meow meow

I met these guys, I took them in
They seem OK, but I'm the coolest
I got my shades, I got my collar
I got my bowl, I'm a badass

I'm a cat, everywhere
I'm a cat like a prowling bear
I'm a cat, to the core
I'm a cat, listen to me roar
I'm a cat!!!!!!!!!

All right, I'm gonna do a little soft-shoe for you, a tap dance,
four-legged style......

> *I'm a cat, everywhere*
> *I'm a cat like a prowling bear*
> *I'm a cat, to the core*
> *I'm a cat, listen to me roar*
> *I'm a cat!!!!!!!!*

The crowd roared.

EPILOGUE

The captain paced back and forth along the gently curved wall that often served as a projection screen but was now a simple white surface. He had called all the parties together in the largest of his meeting spaces, but it hadn't seemed to help anything.

As he paced, his footsteps fell heavily against the tiling.

The tips of his fingers rubbed absently against the bony eye ridges of Lillykins the Shu-shu iguana as the creature rode in the crook of one arm.

Secret Agent Mann sat at one side of the table, which was formed in an egg-shaped oval, farthest from the screen. His blue suit would look unremarkable out in public, but now that James knew Mann was with the GBI, it seemed to totally narc him out.

Lyn and James were across from Mann, but filling seats toward the middle of the expanse.

Frisky, who had finally managed to groom himself clean of von Waschenkaten's Smart Dust, lay regally at the center of the table, his tail languidly beating a slow, random rhythm that was perfectly timed to draw attention. The cat was different now, James thought when he looked at Frisky. Even given his cat nature, the air of intense superiority had been amped by an essence of elite intellectual excellence that was impossible to describe.

Frisky could stare a steady stream of insults at you, but at the same time, you knew he was right.

All the time.

It was a wicked combination.

That said, the cat was good at the poker table now, and that was excellent for making rent. He particularly enjoyed roulette, too, but that was mostly so he could chase the little ball around the table.

Two security systems held the Hedgehog musicians clamped in place, the bassist directly across from Lyn, the washboard player to her right.

Args von Waschenkaten sat the long way across from Secret Agent Mann, stewing. His spindly fingers quietly drummed on the tabletop. His blue-tinted skin seemed darker than it had before, and it served to bring out the undertones of the orange hair he'd so carefully coifed.

His assistant was absent today.

From the way the captain was pacing, James could tell he was embarrassed.

Who wouldn't be?

After losing control of a galactic cruiser full of high-paying customers on a well-publicized jaunt through the stars, the media pressure had to be intense and threatening to get worse before it got better. Just how many diamonds can the incinerated carbon in one captain yield, James thought as he sat back to take in the show.

He was happy he wasn't the one responsible this time.

Or, more properly, thankful it wasn't *Lyn* who was responsible.

Not directly, anyway.

Sure, Lyn's cat had gotten into the thick of things, but you'd be hard-pressed to lay blame on Lyn. Lyn's *cat* was different from Lyn himself. That was James's story, anyway, and with Frisky breaking into long, multi-technical soliloquies like he was a nuclear scientist with a minor in existential philosophy, it wasn't a hard sell.

If James wasn't involved to a degree, he supposed it might even be funny to listen to Frisky call everything "a real cat-ass-trophy" before going into another long dissertation on the inner workings of a star core or the reason a grasshopper leg has micro-hairs over ninety percent of its existence.

Unfortunately, James wasn't completely uninvolved.

Since everyone considered Frisky to belong to Lyn, and since James and Lyn were inseparable in the eyes of the public, there was no getting away from the publicity comet that was blazing over their metaphorical sky. Besides, the cat still considered the brothers' food dispenser to be something of his own, and since his transition into whatever he was now, he expected service to be up to a newfound set of standards.

"You can talk now," James had said while getting

ready for bed last night. "So we can key it to your voice."

"Nah," Frisky had replied with a contented burp over a half-filled plate of meats. "Everything tastes better when you do the work."

Yes, the cat was a real pain in the ass.

Regardless, the captain was not happy.

"Explain it all to me again," the captain said, "but do it real slow like."

"It's quite simple, really," Secret Agent Mann said, standing up again and matching the captain's pace step for step, but in the back of the room rather than the front.

"Somebody stole the spacecraft out from under me. I'm sure it is *not* simple," the captain replied, sternly.

"Ah, yes," Mann said, clearly taking the reprimand. "It's not at all simple! Otherwise, it would never have happened under your watch. Of course! Of course! That much has to be true."

He continued his diligent pacing, one step before the next, slowly, and as if in deep contemplation. And as he paced, the agent cupped his biological hand over the metallic compound of his chin and rubbed it. His eyes narrowed as if in deep contemplation.

James couldn't help but wonder if something was wrong with the agent.

He'd been oddly weird the entire session. Eccentric in ways he wouldn't expect a stodgy cybernetic agent of the GBI would be.

"But the facts, when removed from all the lies," Mann said jauntily, sticking a metallic index finger into the air, "must therefore be the facts, and we can't forget that the facts in this case now include those that say the full truth, the real truth, and nothing but the truth, so help me Mother Murphy—and that this truth says that, while they can certainly lay down a great blues line, these Hedgehogs are *not* just simple blues players! They are, considering these facts that are facts and cannot be refuted, and in light of a series of encrypted searches of the Multiplanet Association of Law Enforcement Services, members of the notorious galactic mafia, which is a collective network of crooks and criminals that have low people in high places across the known universe."

"Indubitably so!" Lyn said, eyes wide in a way that mocked the agent.

Mann seemed to deflate just a little. His jaw churned, but nothing came out.

James boggled at the agent's vocabulary, but saw his discomfort, too. The man was clearly channeling something, though what it might be seemed jumbled and arcane. All James could say for sure was that he might never get the smell of peppermint that was rolling off the agent out of his clothes.

"Could you be a little more direct, Agent Mann?" the captain said.

"I don't think that's possible," Frisky replied. "Mr. Mann is partially human, after all, and we all know what they say about the difference between a cat and a human."

The captain paused in mid-iguana-scratch to give an expectant gaze.

The Shu-shu flickered a tongue at Frisky as if to say *go on.*

"A human always lands on their face," Frisky said, then stretched out one languid claw to check his talon.

"That's horrible," the captain said. "And it doesn't even apply."

"Tough room," Frisky replied, then licked his claw.

At the end of his pacing path, Secret Agent Mann—now ignoring both Lyn's comment and Frisky's attempt at humor—turned on his heel and once again raised a long index finger as if to make a point.

"And we must surmise, now that we understand it to be fact, that these *faux*-Hedgehogs did indeed come onto the gloriously named *Marvel* with intent to connect with Dr. von Waschenkaten, who they had earlier duped into carting aboard an entire crate of their magic dust!"

"It is not magic, and I was not duped!"

Mann whirled on the veterinarian. "You mean to admit that you're a *willing* participant in this intergalactic crime ring?"

"I am no such thing. I didn't even know such a thing existed until a moment ago."

"I told you he was too dense to be a bad guy," Frisky said to James.

"And my invention is Smart Dust. *Not* magic!" von Waschenkaten continued.

"As if you'd know what smart is," the washboard player said, sneering. "I've had enough of your pompous idiocy, Doctor. You're nothing but a fool. Your invention isn't even yours!"

The captain broke in, focused once again on Secret Agent Mann. "So, you're saying the galactic mafia used Dr. von Waschenkaten as a mule?"

"More of a jackass," the washboard player said. "But, sure. Whatever."

"That is the correct inference you are getting, Captain," Mann replied brightly. "They funded Dr. von Waschenkaten because he was easy to … um … lead astray."

"Hey!" the veterinarian said, but then sat back and stewed quietly.

"If the shoe fits you must admit!" Mann called, quieting the dissent.

"I still don't understand," Lyn said.

Frisky flicked his tail hard against the table. "Come on, man, get with it," he growled with exasperation. "We've got better things to do, so just say it already: As far as the mob was concerned, von Waschenkaten was a perfect mark. Too full of himself. Fully ready to be manipulated. They had developed this Smart Dust themselves but didn't have an obvious way to get it into the mainstream, so they needed someone they could fool into thinking he'd developed a way to link into brains. That's what Smart Dust does. Creates pathways into brains."

"Of course, that's what it does, you idiot cat," von Waschenkaten said. "I *told* everyone that!"

Frisky's front paws extended to reveal sharp points.

"Watch it there, Fido. You've got a tongue fancy enough for a scratching-post convention, and I'm willing to check it out."

Von Waschenkaten sat back, lips pressed tight.

Frisky continued. "Of course, that's what you told everyone—but you only knew a little piece of the catnip. *You* told everyone it linked to auditory channels and tongue synapses. But I can tell you from experience up-close and personal, buddy, that the full story is a whale of a lot bigger than that. *Neener, neener, neener,* right? Turns out you didn't develop anything. You just thought you did. I've linked into every piece of data you've ever taken. The timeline fits perfectly. It's all there. You made all your progress after your assistant came in to 'document' your brilliance. But he's the one that did all the work, and what they gave you was already functioning."

"I'll sue you for libel!"

"Sue away, good doctor," Secret Agent Mann broke in. "The facts of the facts remain even after all the lies have been redacted and removed, what the cute little warrior kitty says is spot-on! The truth is that all the progress in your laboratory happened after your trusty assistant arrived and gave you his invisible hand of guidance. Until then, you'd been drifting through one quack plan after another. That's why the good captain there has mister assistant man in a high-security cell as we speak."

For a moment, it appeared von Waschenkaten was going to double down.

Argue. Complain.

Then a welling of tears came to his eyes, and his fashionable shoulders slumped down. He bent over and put his head in his thin hands, then lowered it to the tabletop. "I talked to cats," von Waschenkaten said in a wailing tone. "I talked to Mandruvian goats. I haggled with platypi and garglehogs! Gossiped with Floradian anemone and took tea with the hawks on Hebron B! No one, and I mean no one," he clenched his fist against the tabletop, "can take that away from me!"

"Nice one there, Dr. Seuss," Frisky said.

"It's not just a language pill, you idiot!" the washboard player snapped. "If you'd just shut up and played along, everything would have been fine. But no. You had to go make that public display, didn't you? What a useless diva of a veterinarian you turned out to be. Couldn't even manage to euthanize a damned cat."

"Don't say that word," Frisky warned.

"What word?" the washboard player said, getting his bearings back.

The two exchanged long stares before the Hedgehog blinked.

"Never try to stare down a cat!" Frisky quipped.

He turned his stare to the captain.

"What Secret Agent Mann would be saying right now if he could stop with the blabbering and get down to business is that this Smart Dust is much bigger than a way to talk to animals—or anyone else for that matter. Hell, the world already has base translators for a couple of thousand languages across the galaxy, and us cats have gotten along fine not talking to anyone for a long time, thank you very much—though it would be great if we could work the doors and the meats dispensers."

Frisky paused but went on when no one reacted.

"What the distinguished orator Mann doesn't fully know yet—because how could he, with his out-of-date circuitry and less than optimal human brainwork—is that this was just a test run. Scientists under the intergalactic mob's control created the stuff specifically with the intent to release it into the atmosphere of every planet in the known galaxy. They dumped all that Smart Dust into ventilation ducts planning to put the crew and passengers under their control, thereby taking over the cruiser. If it worked, they would do it around the universe."

"These are mad people," Secret Agent Mann said.

The veterinarian stammered, sitting up and shaking his head as he gained a full understanding of the stakes of this game. "No! That can't be," he finally said.

It was almost enough to make James feel sorry for the sot.

Idiot.

"If you control vacuum, you control the world," Frisky said.

"I still don't understand," Lyn said, stretching back and scratching the top of his head. "If von Waschenkaten was such a hack, how did he get first billing as keynote speaker for the entire cruise?"

The door swiped open then, and in stepped Asa Roumie, the entertainment director, her hair dyed white and her fashionable scarf of fuchsia and blue flowing behind.

"There you are!" she screamed, pointing at the boys. She stepped into the room far enough to let the door close behind her—which it did with a soft swoosh.

She gathered herself.

"Complaints are rolling in, Captain. These two broke their contract by stopping their show—in mid-song, I hear! I demand you throw those two into the brig."

"What?" Lyn said.

"Several of the attendees of last night's event said so."

"You've got to be kidding me."

Roumie stepped around the table.

"I am most definitely not kidding!" She commanded the projector on, and a display sprang up with three signed affidavits. "Arrest them now, and I'll begin their discharge paperwork."

James sat back abruptly. "I think you're too late, Director Roumie," he said.

"What do you mean?"

James swiveled his gaze.

"Yes, Captain, I think you do need to arrest someone here, but it's not us." He turned back to Roumie. "The entertainment director here spent a long time telling us exactly how hard she worked to convince the good Dr. von Wakiwaki to come here—I'd bet even going so far as to cross a few ethical lines that the press would be interested in hearing about. Wouldn't you think it strange for an established entertainment director to go so far out of her way to include a hack like von Waschenwaschen onto the show log? And just who do you think booked the Hedgehogs in right beside him."

"Coincidence?" Lyn chimed in.

"I think not," James replied.

"Don't be stupid, kid," Roumie said.

"I'm not."

Frisky jumped in. "The boys are right," he replied. "I wouldn't have thought to look at her at all, but I just rifled through her system and it's all there. And it makes sense. Asa Roumie is on the mob's payroll. She booked von Katenwasher on purpose, and she's due a cut after the cruise returns. Already set up a secret bank account off the star grid to take the money. Plans to retire early and fraternize with a never-ending series of cabana boys who are adroit at closing their eyes and holding their noses as they serve Sonderport daiquiris and whatever else money can buy."

Secret Agent Mann did a double take. "Yes," he said. "That does make sense. For a cat, you're a genius."

"Thank you," Frisky said, taking an exaggerated bow. "That's saying a lot."

"We need you in the agency," Mann said.

"Har!" Frisky replied. "A cat's place is in the spotlight!"

"I see." Mann sighed. "Thank you anyway. If you ever change your mind, let me know. Your work has helped me save my career. I'll be honored to go to the mats for you."

"Will do, Mr. Magoo."

Secret Agent Mann continued. "I do need to arrest this woman, though, Captain," he said, pointing to Roumie.

"Not a problem," the captain said. "I've already called security."

He paused his iguana-scratching. The Shu-shu stared hard at him.

"The only thing I don't understand is this," he said. "If all that Smart Dust made everyone go crazy and fall into the mob's mind control, why not Frisky?"

Frisky gave a throaty guffaw.

"Come on, Cappy! Get with the program! You know damned well that *nobody* can tell a cat what to do."

Everyone in the room laughed, even von Waschenkaten.

"Well," James said. "All this excitement has been fun, but we've got a gig to play tonight, and we need our rest."

Lillykins tilted her head and whipped out a sliver of her tongue.

Frisky stood up and stretched.

"About that," Frisky said. "I had a good time with my song in there last night. Since it looks like a slot's opened up at the Top Cat, I was figuring I'd step in. I've already jotted down a few ditties I'd like to try out."

"That would be great," the captain said, glancing at the Hedgehogs. "We're going to need another act to finish the cruise."

"You play the blues, too?" Secret Agent Mann said, suddenly even more starstruck at Frisky's presence.

"I was born to sing the blues," Frisky said. "When it comes to pain and suffering, I'm your cat."

"I think I'm in love."

"I need a backup band, though." Frisky turned to the boys. "I hear the Intergalactic Band of Brilliance can play a lick or two. Do you two got it in ya to pull two shows in a night?"

Lyn chuckled.

"Us?" James said. "Back you?"

"I'm the cat, man." Frisky sat upright and puffed his chest out. "And I'm the one that brought down the house last night."

The Moore brothers exchanged glances.

"He has a point," Lyn said.

"Yeah, I hate it when he's right." James looked at

Frisky, who returned the gaze with a content smugness. "And it's even worse when he doesn't talk."

The captain laughed and scratched the Shu-shu again. "Thank goodness my little Lillykins can't talk."

The lizard slipped its tongue out to taste the air again, and James was certain little Lillykins locked gazes with Frisky. A silent shudder crossed James's spine.

"Let me ask, too," the captain said. "The Hedgehogs were going to headline our next cruise. I don't have an entertainment director to fix the problem right now, so if we double your fee, could you stick around and play the next tour? It's the Magical Mystery Cruise, so that should be fun at least. Full of magicians."

"We'll need triple," Frisky said.

"Triple?"

"It's a good deal, man. You're getting two acts for the price of one."

The captain pursed his lips, then looked at the brothers.

"It's a deal if you want it."

James hung his head. He looked at Lyn who, by whatever powers that be, had managed not to simply agree on the spot. "I hate to say it," James muttered. "But it seems too good to pass up."

"It's a deal, then," Lyn called.

"Outstanding," the captain said. "I'll have my admin write up the contracts."

With that, the gathering split up, the Hedgehogs and Entertainment Director Roumie being escorted to the brig, and von Waschenkaten sent off to be interrogated by Secret Agent Mann (and Mann promising to show up for Frisky's jam).

Frisky left to walk his property.

The boys strode down the hallway by themselves.

"What are the odds?" Lyn said.

"What's that?"

"Two straight cruises, two straight intergalactic crime rings."

"Yeah, that is weird."

"I mean, what are the odds, right?"

"Yeah," James said. "What are the odds?"

He took in his walking,-gravity-well of a problem-attractor brother who, it seemed, had a not-so-hidden superpower geared toward finding himself in the middle of all chaos.

"Well, at least the next cruise on our contract should be easy."

"Yeah," James replied. "A five-day tour for magicians. Should be interesting."

"Yeah," Lyn said as they neared their cabin. "And what could go wrong on a ship full of magicians?"

YOU'VE REACHED
THE END!

We hope you've enjoyed the raucous cruise through the galaxy! If you have, you might find other books in the series to be equally as fun.

Also, if you enjoyed this book, your review on the book retailer of your choice is a great way to help us out. Even a quick line or two can help!

Thank you so much for reading our work!

ACKNOWLEDGMENTS

We would like to thank all the people who have helped us make it this far in life—but, man, that would be a nearly infinite list. Instead, let's narrow it a little. Thanks to all the sets of Collins brothers who came before us. Thanks to Dad, especially, for hanging around while we were brainstorming a bit.

Thanks, too, to Kristine Kathryn Rush, Dean Wesley Smith, and Lisa Silverthorne for throwing their own ideas at us when we asked for a bit of advice. That was a fun lunch.

Thanks to our beta readers, Sharon Bass and John Bodin. You two are the bestest.

Thanks, also, to Karen and Lisa for not laughing at us when we decided to take a flier at this silliness—with special focus on Lisa for being our last reader!

And, finally, thanks to the many airplanes that flew over our recording studio as we were grabbing the audio version of this book. Or, um, actually, no thanks there. Those planes were a real pain.

ABOUT RON & JEFF COLLINS

Jeff and Ron Collins—the original Cruise Brothers—first played music together as youthful teens down in the basement of their home in Louisville, Kentucky. (*"No grass, but a lotta grapes!"* - inside Mom joke, there). While occasionally annoying the family and their beloved cat Frisky with boisterous songs at 2am, there were some gems that have managed to stand the test of time (a few even found their way into this Cruise Brothers series).

Then Jeff fiddled around with theater and improv comedy before hightailing it out to Los Angeles to become a rock star, and Ron found his way through engineering and into the life of a high-powered icon in the science fiction field.

Or something like that.

Now here they are. Back, better than ever.

Aside from composing and producing original works, these days you can find Jeff playing live with several tribute bands, including a tribute to Genesis (Gabble Ratchet), Alice Cooper (Pretties For You), and Jane's Addiction (Jane's Addicted).

Ron's short fiction has received a Writers of the Future prize and a CompuServe HOMer Award. His short story "The White Game" was nominated for the Short Mystery Fiction Society's 2016 Derringer Award.

With his daughter, Brigid, he edited the anthology *Face the Strange.*

You can follow Ron at his website: Typosphere.com
Or join Ron's Readers and get two free books!
typosphere.com / newsletter /

ALSO BY RON COLLINS

<u>Novels</u>

Stealing the Sun (9 books)

Saga of the God-Touched Mage (8 books)

Fairies & Fastballs w/Brigid Collins (3 books)

The PEBA Diaries (2 books)

The Knight Deception

Wakers

<u>Collections</u>

Holiday Hope

They Came Back

Collins Creek (Vol 1) Contemporary Currents and Historical Eddies

Collins Creek (Vol 2) Streams of Speculation

Collins Creek (Vol 3) Tides of Adventure

Tomorrow in All the Worlds

Picasso's Cat & Other Stories

Five Magics

<u>Novella</u>

The Bridge to Fae Realm

<u>Poetry</u>

Five Seven Five (100 SF Haiku)